Born in Oamaru, Fiona Farrell was educated at Otago and Toronto where she graduated in drama. She has published two collections of poetry, two collections of short stories and four novels, three of which have been shortlisted for the Montana New Zealand Book Awards. *The Skinny Louie Book* won the award in 1992, while *The Hopeful Traveller* (2001) and the popular *Book Book* (2004) were also nominated for the international IMPAC Award. Her poetry and short stories have been widely anthologised. She has received the Bruce Mason Award for Playwrights, the Katherine Mansfield Fellowship in Menton, and in 2006 spent six months in Donoughmore, Ireland, as one of the inaugural recipients of the Rathcoola Residency for New Zealand and Australian writers and artists. *Mr Allbones' Ferrets* was completed while she was in Ireland.

Mr Allbones' Ferrets

an historical
pastoral satirical scientifical
romance, with mustelids

FIONA FARRELL

𝒱
VINTAGE

This book has been written with the assistance of the Rathcoola Residency, Donoughmore, Eire. Thanks to Maryrose Crook for the detail from the Pest Dress.

A catalogue record for this book is available from the National Library of New Zealand.

A VINTAGE BOOK
published by
Random House New Zealand
18 Poland Road, Glenfield, Auckland,
New Zealand
www.randomhouse.co.nz

Random House International
Random House
20 Vauxhall Bridge Road
London, SW1V 2SA
United Kingdom

Random House Australia (Pty) Ltd
20 Alfred Street, Milsons Point, Sydney,
New South Wales 2061,
Australia

Random House South Africa Pty Ltd
Isle of Houghton
Corner Boundary Road and Carse
   O'Gowrie
Houghton 2198,
South Africa

Random House Publishers India
   Private Ltd
301 World Trade Tower, Hotel
   Intercontinental Grand Complex,
Barakhamba Lane, New Delhi 110 001,
India

First published 2007

© 2007 Fiona Farrell

The moral rights of the author have been asserted

ISBN 978 1 86941 864 9

Design: Elin Bruhn Termannsen
Cover painting: Detail from *The Sorrowful Eye: Pest Dress* by Maryrose Crook © 2004
Cover design: Katy Yiakmis
Author photo: Juliet Nicholas
Printed in Australia by Griffin Press

To Ursula, Susannah and Doug, as always.
And to Robyn Carrig and the Rathcoola Residency,
with thanks and affection.

We can so far take a prophetic glance into futurity as to foretell that it will be the common and widely-spread species, belonging to the larger and dominant groups, which will ultimately prevail and procreate new and dominant species. As all the living forms of life are the lineal descendants of those which lived long before the Silurian epoch, we may feel certain that the ordinary succession by generation has never once been broken, and that no cataclysm has desolated the whole world. Hence, we may look with some confidence to a secure future of equally appreciable length. And as natural selection works solely by and for the good of each being, all corporeal and mental endowments will tend to progress towards perfection.

Charles Darwin, *The Origin of Species*, 1859

1.

	£	s	d
350 ferrets, weasels and stoats	70	0	0
Cost of food before shipment	135	15	0
Collecting labour etc.	16	5	0
Sundry accounts	69	8	5
2750 pigeons	120	6	3
Travelling expenses etc.	4	4	3
Ditto	2	3	9
450 pigeons	19	13	9
Food for pigeons	42	4	6
Shipping charges	6	4	3
Tarpaulins	8	17	2
Deck houses and fittings	54	3	0
Freight	94	10	0
Passage money and ship's outfit	16	0	0
	659	15	4

May 1885 account, Riddiford Papers, New Zealand National Library

He stands in the dark, shoulders hunched, hands shoved deep in his pockets, the air poking chilly little fingers through rips and tears to bare skin. He wriggles his toes in thin boots, keeps a sharp ear cocked for the snuffling of a dog, the rustling of dead leaves that could mean detection: that he's been spotted and stands at that instant like some unwary beast, poised between the beads on the foretip of the keeper's gun. Beyond the crowd of trees just breaking into leaf a bird calls, over and over, a peculiar plaintive *whoop whoop* he does not recognise. The stars hang brilliant between the branches, a wide daisy-field of light. Bright enough to see by, though the moon has dwindled to a scraping. Bright enough to make out the belly hump of the warren among fronds of bracken and the pale web of his nets, knitted, he hopes, to cover every exit.

He stretches full length and, with his ear pressed against the swelling of the earth, he can hear the usual murmurings: things growing and things easing through narrow crevices, mingled with the rush of his own blood and the soft footfall of his own beating heart. And then, from somewhere yards below as he lies listening like a baby at the breast, there rise other sounds: the brush of something squeezing through a shaft, its fur burnishing clay, the sudden *thump thump thump* of the alarum, a rapid scrabbling, a muffled chorus of squeals, the drumming accelerating to a frantic tattoo.

Down there in the dark there's something approaching fast, red eyes glistening down the length of a tunnel, and there is no alternative but flight, abandoning offspring like a cluster of pink cherries in the nest, to bolt for the open or, if that is too distant, to scramble into the nearest stop, head wedged against a blind wall, haunches to the intruder. Safe, the rabbit hopes, from attack. Brain and eyes tucked securely beyond reach.

But in Pinky, the rabbit has met its match. Pinky, her tail brisk as a brush with the pure joy of killing. Pinky, bred small to squeeze through the merest gap. Pinky, who can reach the goal denied other more massively built members of her kind: the base of the skull or the glistening circle of the rabbit's eye, protuberant with terror, where she can wriggle close and deliver the death thrust, neat and sure. Where she can claim the delicacy prized above all others: the creature's brain, soft and fragrant as whipped cream, sucked from the cranial bowl. With the promise of such pleasure, Pinky will not be deterred should the rabbit be jammed tight. If there is indeed no gap, even for her slight frame, she'll simply scrape every vestige of fur from the creature's rear and make a start while it still lives, severing the tendons connecting the spine to the back legs. She'll nibble a little perhaps, just for the taste, then move on, leaving the rabbit paralysed, trapped and bloody while she attends to whatever else lives in the bury, bolting the lot for the freedom they assume lies only in the open air, at the surface.

Allbones can hear her at it, sleek and swift, twisting and turning in a tight tunnel as if her body were not composed of bone but were sinew alone and malleable cartilage. She moves with speed and daunting purpose through the vast network below ground, for the warren is ancient, a kingdom of dark tunnels stretching for who knows how many acres in the light, dry soils. Once it was tended, for the silvery rabbit skins earned a good price from hatters in London, but fashions change, and the rabbits have had it to themselves for years now, laying claim to a wide territory, their burrows stretching so far beneath furze and bracken that no one can quite say where they might end.

There's a frenzy of scratching, of scrabbling, of distant squealing, the high pitch of terror rising toward the surface. Allbones straightens quickly and leaps to his feet in a single bound as the first rabbit hurtles forth from the earth and tangles in the net. The pegs hold, driven in as hard as he could manage and booted home. And the drawstrings run true, pursing as they are intended to, around a big buck. Allbones makes a grab for him before he can tangle his net into a bramble thicket of muddied hemp it will take hours to sort. Stinking of fear, hind legs flailing for purchase, claws extended, the buck screams, his call curiously identical to the cry of a frantic child. Allbones takes swift hold of the legs and feels for the light bones of the neck. A stretch, a twist and it's done. The buck gives one final mighty kick, then flops into a twitchy death. But already there's another, bolting from a hole a couple of yards distant beneath the roots of an old oak, so Allbones lets the buck drop (a good weight, not too old, and the thin membrane of his ears has torn readily so his flesh will still be tender) and takes the second. A doe at the very point of kindle with a cargo of kits seething in her belly, and she is shrieking as if tonight were Armageddon, which in a way it is, from the rabbits' point of view.

The tug, the twist. A scrabbling at his feet and there's another. And another. They're running in all directions, dragging at his nets. It's a mayhem of thrashing bodies, all rabbits from the sound of it, no indigent rats driven from borrowed sanctuary and primed to bite, as only a doe rat can, at an unwary hand. No fox seeking sanctuary in the bury, no wild cat thinking herself safely curled away from marauding toms to give birth to her young. Tonight is all rabbits. Allbones runs from one to another, the sweat breaking out beneath his heavy coat, his breathing becoming laboured as he tries to muffle all their cries before the sound can carry to the groundsman's ears, for sounds carry far on such still nights in early spring when there is a lingering memory of frost in the air. He tugs and twists and, when he has time, disentangles each creature, then drops it into one of the pockets sewn into the lining of his coat, until the garment hangs warm and heavy from his narrow shoulders.

The flurry begins to ease.

One more rabbit, under the brambles.

A pause.

Another.

Then silence. No more scrabbling, no budging at the net.

And where is Pinky?

It is time to move now, to furl the nets quickly into a figure of eight around finger and thumb, then a neat twist of the drawstring to tie them fast for another night. It's time to count them all off, to make sure none have been missed in the dark, before slipping them one by one into his pockets, along with the pegs and the graft he uses for digging. Everything stowed away safe from inspection beneath the bulky worsted of his old coat. The rabbits lie cradled between death and that lifetime of sweet nibbled grass on dewy mornings, play on a twilit hillside, the soft nest of milky kits. He smooths the earth where he has been at work this evening, carefully bending back the fonds of bracken to conceal his activities, and all the while he is keeping an eye out for Pinky.

Where is she?

It is time to be off, with full pockets, before it is too late and the luck of the evening runs dry. The big house beyond the trees stands empty — has been empty for over a year, according to Mother Mossop, fount of all gossip. Ever since old Mr Aubrey's demise. 'And not before time,' she had said, squinting to fill a quart bottle with a thin trickle of her beet brandy. 'He were that near, he'd not part wi' his own droppin's.'

The house may be unoccupied but some staff have stayed on, including the groundsman, a short-legged former infantryman with some Irish regiment who had learned out in India to shoot fast and accurately. Allbones has seen him once or twice about Ledney, keeping himself to himself and meeting nobody's eye, and he has no wish to make his closer acquaintance. Particularly not tonight. He kneels again and places his ear to the ground, but there is no sound.

Silence.

Pinky is not normally given to lying up, casually devouring her kill below ground while he hops from foot to foot overhead in his thin and leaking boots. He has had her from birth and she has never let him down. He has taken pains with her, gentled her, fed her on dabs of his own spit which she lapped from the palm of his hand, and in return she has rewarded him with rabbit and rat and never once left him as she is leaving him tonight, target for the groundsman. He has been careful always, of course, and never entered her to the warren without taking the precaution of feeding her well first. Tonight she has had a plump rat, taken fresh from beneath Mother Mossop's pigpen. He nipped off the tail to preserve her from the mange then gave it to her and she sighed and squeaked with the pleasure of a warm cadaver all to herself. He gave her water, too, a full measure, as it is hot work below ground, killing. He has never subscribed to the theory that a ferret will work better on an empty belly, though there are plenty who do: Fowler Metcalfe, for example, who sends his ferrets in hungry with their lips sewn shut in a makeshift muzzling. Fowler boasts that his tallies speak for the efficacy of hunger. But Fowler has always been a fat boaster and a liar to boot. Allbones doubts his reports, his three hundred and eighty rabbits in one night from a single warren over Brinkton way, his one hundred and twenty rats in half an hour.

Allbones feeds his ferrets well and his ferrets bolt rabbits, rather than lying up to feed below ground, and he has never lost a single one.

Until, perhaps, tonight.

Pinky has had her rat and she has been watered well so it is unlikely she is down there feasting. Not that she would pass up the chance of a kit or two, naked and succulent and sweet as mother's milk. But they would not detain her long in the joy of the chase. A quick gulp in passing, as a man might snap a handful of plums from a wayside tree.

Allbones kneels in the starlight, his breath misting to a little cloud about his shoulders. The air about the warren stinks of blood, musk, fear, a smell so pungent that it could surely alert an attentive dog a quarter mile distant. It's a good half-hour since the last rabbit bolted into the web and his waiting hand. From beyond the woods he can hear the dull clang of the Ledney clock. He counts off the strokes. Eleven. Time to be gone. He presses his ear to the damp earth and hears nothing. Silence. The silence that falls when a crowded room has emptied suddenly. The silence that falls over a bloodied field after battle.

He wishes desperately for his white hob. Pompey was big and strong and trained to the line. With Pompey in his pocket he could have taken action now: he could have entered him into the warren to search, dragging the line between tree roots and broken rock through the network of tunnels below ground. Pompey would have sought out Pinky. He would find and stay and, after a few hours of desperate digging, Allbones could conceivably have traced them both, drawn them forth and brought them home again.

But Pompey has gone. Or, more correctly, he has been taken. The white polecat hob for whom Allbones traded half his stock one afternoon at the rat pit at the King's Arms. Pompey was admittedly no fighter. He proved himself timid in the pit up against a big buck rat that fought savagely and beat him off, along with two other hobs, before one of Fowler's sluts dealt death like a dancer. Allbones wanted the white hob nevertheless and afterwards, as the bets were being settled, he got him: a breeder, vigorous to mate, who had to be removed from the barrel when the sluts were in season or he would forget to eat and lose condition entirely. Who mounted them all, every slut in the barrel, not once but several times over, then took the young hobs too, and kits so young they still had their eyes closed so that they left the nest already impregnated with the seed which, when they were old enough and when the season was right, burst into young. Pompey mounted them all, chattering happily for an hour or more at a time while paws and teeth scratched bare patches in their fur, and anchored so firmly by his thrusting prick that the pair could be lifted clear from the floor yet remain coupled. Allbones held them in his hand and observed the hob at close quarters. Pompey's eyes glazed with lust and his body rippled in ecstatic spasm. Allbones observed his ardour with wonder mixed with not a little admiration.

The big white hob had repaid Allbones' investment by

fathering a numerous brood of kits as lithe and strong as himself and, as often as not, pure white. A rich creamy white easy to spot out in the woods on a dark night, a white that made Allbones' kits the best of their kind for miles around. By ruthlessly culling any sandie or poley, Allbones had achieved perfection: a stock of pure whites, noted for their strength, agility and beauty, and the whitest of all, the most elegant, the most perfect, was Pinky. Sharp of muzzle, fearless, fierce and generally reliable.

But not tonight. Allbones stands abandoned in the dark, the trophies of the evening stiffening in his coat pockets, and curses. Curses the loss of his white hob, curses himself for drawing Pinky from the barrel tonight, rather than Flick or Fluff. He had been eager to make a start as night fell, to escape the cramped room where the littl'uns had squabbled and tumbled underfoot all day, no matter where he had tried to sit to mend his nets. The cramped cottage hummed with restlessness after days, weeks of rain: rain like the rain that had caused them to build the ark in the Bible. Forty days and forty nights of grey rain driving in from the east with the chill of the steppes still on its breath, rain that swelled every ditch to a stream, every stream to a mighty torrent, rain that melted lanes to knee-deep mud and flooded fields so that the cattle stood lowing piteously for rescue on diminishing islands as the water took back what it had surrendered only a few decades before to the inventive engineer.

Rain that made all outdoor employment impossible. Allbones, like all the other day labourers and bankin-men, sat idle, the banks and ditches where they earned their daily keep drowned and barely holding their own against the churning floods of muddy ochre. Rain gurgled in the gutters; no work, no pay. Rain drip drip dripped through every hole and cranny in wall or roof so that nothing could be kept dry. The flour would swell and rot, the walls would sprout a furry coat of mould, and soon the coughing would start, the Ledney Carol: a paroxysm of spit and suffocating phlegm followed as like as not by pallor, wasting, and the spatter of blood flowering like poppies on the pillow.

But today, a miracle! Mid-afternoon, the rain ceased. A pale shaft of sunlight fell in the door when it was opened to the yard and the littl'uns tumbled out to meet it, into a world new-washed, webbed with raindrops and gloriously muddy. Allbones, too, made ready, eager for the silence of the woods, for the night wind furtive among the branches, for the scratching of rabbits tangled in his nets. And eager, too, for meat. Meat boiled, meat fried. Liver and kidneys and brains and plump thighs and bones to suck bare after weeks of turnip filched from the barn behind the church, or potatoes lifted one at a time from Mother Mossop's jealously guarded store. And nothing to lend them savour except a few thrushes taken from their sodden nests in the hedgerow, their boney carcasses exuding the merest hint of sustenance. All afternoon Allbones' mouth had run wet at the thought of meat. His tongue had swollen thick at the thought of meat. And just as soon as the sun wavered down between racks of uncertain crimson, he was off, thrusting his hand into the barrel behind the door where he had moved his ferrets from the yard after Pompey's myste-rious disappearance. And he had drawn forth Pinky.

She snapped at his hand as she usually did, not liking to be woken from her warm straw bed, but he placated her with the rat and tucked her into his coat pocket, the tiny *slup slup slup* of her teeth gnawing at a bone a happy accompaniment as he escaped the clamour of the cottage for the solitude of Ledney Wood.

Standing out here in the dark though, he wishes his hand had alighted on one of Pinky's siblings: Flick or Fluff were not as brave as she, being older and more cautious, but they were utterly reliable. They would never leave a fellow in the lurch, target for any shotgun that happened to be in the vicinity. He should have taken Flick.

He should have picked out Fluff.

For the third time, he counts his nets.

Eight.

As usual.

He stamps his frozen feet.

He bends down and drums his fingers at the burrow entrance, hoping that the sound might intrigue her, wherever she is, and that she might be drawn forth to investigate.

Nothing.

He takes his knife and quickly guts the smallest rabbit, tipping the tangled knot, steaming and pungent, at the burrow entrance, hoping the smell might draw her forth.

Nothing.

He tramps down the brambles, wondering if he has indeed covered all the exits. Perhaps there is one he has missed? Thorns tear at hands and face and catch in his clothing, ripping flesh and cloth. Perhaps the warren extends much further than he has reckoned? Perhaps she has emerged already from some concealed point? Perhaps she is at this very moment racing for some duckpond or some farmwife's treasured poultry pen to wreak havoc among the dozing denizens? The kind of havoc that will likely guarantee her own demise in a baited trap. Perhaps his bold white ferret is gone for good.

But suddenly she is there. She sits at the mouth of the main burrow, like milk spilt from the lip of a dark pitcher. She is calmly licking blood from her matted fur. Her bright little eyes look up as he approaches. 'Didn't I do well?' she might be saying, as she takes her sweetmeat: a rabbit's eye popped from the socket, round and fresh and ever so slightly reproachful. She nips his hand once, hard, to make some point about due patience and due respect, then she curls in his pocket to sleep, nose tucked to belly, bloodied paws folded demurely, like a young girl at her first communion.

Allbones buttons his coat, tucking the rabbits in as if they were infants, against the cold. He takes a swig from the flask, a raw spirit Mother Mossop manufactures from the sugar beet and sells surreptitiously. It burns a fiery trail down the gullet. The scent of musk hangs about him, as telltale as if he had hung the rabbits from his belt as trophies, but now, should any late walker chance upon him on the path home, well, he's that layabout from down the Bottom End, drunk again, indulging in some public house while his brothers and sisters lie neglected in a ragged cottage, unfed, unkempt. Hapless orphans in his careless charge.

Let them suppose what they please, thinks Allbones as he beats his way through the bracken to the declivity that marks the route of the old road, overgrown since it was cut by the wall when the land was taken into the big house's holding back sometime. Let them judge and be damned. What others think means nothing to a man whose pockets are stuffed with good meat. Rabbit blood seeps through the lining. Their bodies knock heavily against his thighs.

He moves rapidly, knowing from memory every fallen log and every hollow. The woods smell fresh and green, of damp earth and last season's rotting leaf, and the smell mingles pungently with ferret musk and blood and raw spirit. All around him there is the rustling of other creatures intent upon their own peculiar nocturnal business: hedgehog and badger and mouse and nameless multitudes of insects, snuffling and scratching and coupling. This is the best time, the time when he feels completely at his ease. The woods are as fresh as that place he recalls from the time when he was a lad, and went to Ledney Church with his ma and listened to the man talk of Eden; of all the living things, new made, trying out their legs and wings and voices for the first time, all the flowers unfurling and the trees working out how the seasons should go — bud to blossom to fallen leaf and back again. He'd sat on the hard bench, pressed against his mother's side and sucking on the scrap of broken marmady she'd given to keep him still, imagining it: the birds tottering like bairns from their branches and discovering flight, the fish wriggling in the streams, the animals neighing and barking and mooing, all brand new. It was a childish fantasy, but now that he is grown it still pleases him: this is the Eden time, and he, walking here among the buds of hazel and the little Jack lilies lifting their modest heads from the earth for another season, he, Allbones, is the first man. His body is not bent as it bends to shovel mud or to hoe turnips for pay, but fine and free. He is the first man in the new world. He steps strong and independent along the secret paths he alone knows, emerging just by the gate in the wall, where an owl swoops out of nowhere and brushes his shoulder before disappearing soundlessly among the trees. It feels like a good omen.

The gate is padlocked, of course, and the wall sports an armoury of spikes and broken glass along its crest. At first glance the gate itself is a whimsical medley of cast-iron foliage and fleur de lis, but each little bud doubles as a dagger, each tendril is a prison bar. Allbones, however, knows his way about this cunning jungle. By the bottom left hinge there is one point where the ironwork thins, leaving a gap the maker no doubt believed too small to permit access. He had not reckoned on a lithe young man who, as his mother said, seems to lack a skeleton. A pliable youth, with sinew where others have bone.

He removes his coat and carefully threads it through the gap — rabbits, nets, ferret and all. Then he exhales until he is as small as he can be, bends and twists, arms first, and wriggles his way out, as earlier that evening he wriggled his way in.

'Not Allbones,' his mother used to say, ruffling his hair as he emptied his pockets of some treasure — a cabbage from the walled vicarage garden, a little bag of coal lifted from the locked shed at Brinkton Station, a loaf of bread from a kitchen windowsill, 'but No-bones!' He was her skinny lad, the runt of the litter who had grown quick and cunning and able to squeeze his way through any gap or cranny, scaling soffit and drainpipe, up trees, under hedges. It was his skill, a most particular and valuable talent. 'My young Master No-bones,' she called him.

The knack lay in the breath: when to draw in, when to release, when to stiffen, when to flex. A quick twist past the murderous fleur de lis and he's falling like a newborn calf head-first into a pile of leaves. He lies still for a moment, sniffing the air for the scent of dog or oil on gunstock or the groundsman's peppermint. He listens, too, the tiny canals in his pink ears flaring.

Nothing.

No shocking cacophony of barking, no crack of gunshot, no 'Got you, my lad!' He lets out his breath and re-buttons his coat, and its warmth settles about his shoulders like a defensive second skin.

Out here beyond the wall the woods continue, but here they are on common land, a shrunken remnant of the forest that once sustained a village, where anyone might gather acorns to fatten a pig, or collect wood for their fires. Allbones avoids the road, choosing the old shortcut through the woods. And here, too, he knows every dip and hollow, though beneath the ancient trees all light from the stars is lost. He finds his way by the sound of the path beneath his feet: the crunch of dry leaf on higher ground, the suck of mud where the path skirts the stream, the damp slip of bluebells in a clearing sighing their sweet scent. A hundred yards to go through the wood, then across Mossop's Field and onto the lane where he could be any drunkard, weaving his way from the Lion or the King's Arms, and then he's home.

He has begun to relax, to become careless, for he does not see them at all until he is almost on top of them. One second he is swinging along, the evening's takings cooling in his pockets and his thoughts racing ahead to his triumphant return, the next there's a sudden eruption from beneath his feet, an 'I say! Careful!' He stops in mid-stride, reaching instinctively for the knife in his right pocket. 'Watch where you're going!' says the voice. A man's voice. And though there's a nervous edge to it, for who might this be, stumbling out of the dark, it is nevertheless the kind of voice to be answered with 'sir'.

Allbones regains his balance, thinking quickly as his hand takes firm hold of bone handle and a few inches of Sheffield steel. There is another sharp intake of breath and an 'Oh my!' accompanied by the rustling of petticoats and the distinct whiff of violets. It is not a scent Allbones cares for particularly. Bodies left unburied too long in a warm season stink of violets. The scent rouses the fleeting vision: a dark burrow of a room, his mother laid in a narrow box on an unsteady table, his brothers and sisters standing around with their mouths gaping like so many baby birds, the *tap tap tap* of the nails as the lid is hammered shut, the thud as she is dropped into rough ground, not buried as is proper in the convivial crush about St Peter's Ledney, but abandoned, a white bulb among the weeds beyond the church wall. Wild garlic, cow parsley, and the pallid stink of violets.

No. It is not a scent he favours, and normally he would pick it easily from the bouquet of bluebells and mud and damp spring leaf. But tonight he has been careless and here it is rising to meet him: violets, soap, cigars and port and Macassar. A man and a woman. The man older, the woman — to judge from the girlish pitch to her voice — much younger.

'Beg pardon, sir,' says Allbones.

Up to the usual, he supposes, though it is not normally the ones who smell of port and eau de violette who come here to the woods after dark, but the ones who smell of cramped cottages and boiled cabbage and the mutton reek of cheap tallow candles and clothes that see the inside of a washtub maybe once a year. It's not normal to come across the smell of clean linen in Ledney Wood on a starlit night.

'Pardon, Miss,' he says.

And now the first voice has him: a village lad, Bottom End. It has also perhaps identified the whiff of Mother Mossop's grandly titled 'brandy'. It knows where this interloper belongs in the great scheme of things, and with that knowledge it recovers confidence. It regains its dignity, rising to its full height.

'You clumsy fool!' it says.

'Sorry, sir,' says Walter Allbones with his pockets full of purloined rabbits, enough to take him down for months if not years, to force him from the burrow he shares with his brothers and sisters, to drive them all into further desperate improvisation. Port-and-cigars is standing his ground, now that he is confident it is his to stand on, as it has always been, as it always will be.

'Why don't you look where you're going?'

And why, thinks Allbones, don't you choose somewhere other than what is practically a public highway for your dalliance? Why bring your dolly to what's left of Ledney Wood when you've got the whole of some fancy big house to play in? He can say nothing, of course, not with a couple of dozen rabbits to consider. Keep it mild, keep it calm, keep it, above all, short.

'Didn't see you there, sir,' he says, 'in the dark, like.'

Though it is not in fact quite dark. Now that he is fully alert, he can see there is a dim ruddy glow making strange shadows of tree trunk and fern. There's a lantern on the path at their feet, screened with red paper. How could he not have noticed before?

'Oh!' sighs the girl. 'They've gone! They've disappeared!' And Allbones can see the smudge of her face among the fern on the bank, pale as the petals on some night-blooming flower. 'We were observing the badgers,' she says, as if this were some normal conversation in a well-lit drawing room, as if this stranger blundering out of the dark deserved some explanation.

She scrambles to her feet. 'We'd been waiting for ages,' she says, as if Allbones would care, as if it were any concern of his what a couple of strangers might be up to, out here in Ledney Wood. Kiss and couple and good luck to you both, he is thinking, wanting only to pass and move on, but the path is narrow and she blocks his way, her skirts brushing the undergrowth on either side. The smell of violets is overpowering.

How could he have missed it, and the port, the cigars, the oil of Macassar? The stink of wealth is as strong as the markings of fox or cat. As strong as the musky stink of the badger sett that has been here for as long as Allbones can remember, and a hundred years or more before him no doubt, dug into the bank beneath the remains of some crumbling masonry of unknown provenance. The spoilheap gleams in the dim light, piled several feet high. There's the cheesy reek of badger droppings deposited neatly, as is their wont, a few yards from their door, and the sharper scent of fresh piss on tree bole and stone announcing their territory. He has seen the badgers many times, met the old man boar and his sows snuffling down the path toward the rich worm pickings of Mossop's Field. He has observed them, too, from time to time, watching the old boar cuffing aside the cubs who would one day take his place. One day there would come a young boar strong enough to take him on. They'd circle, the old one stiffer now, less agile, the younger fine and fierce and above all eager to mate. He'd find the weak spot in the old boar, that tender place above the tail where he could get a grip, and then he'd try for the kill. And when the old one was down and bleeding, lying like something discarded, tossed aside like an old boot into the bracken, the young one would take his sows, claiming them one by one. That was the way of nature. Whenever

Allbones came upon the boar with his legs wrapped about a sow's heaving sides, the two of them out in Mossop's Field or on the woodland path, chattering and purring with pleasure, 'You take 'er,' he'd say. 'You take 'er. You've won 'er, fair an' square!'

The girl dusts off her skirts. 'We saw two,' she says. 'But we were waiting for the cubs. My grandfather was certain there would be cubs.' She is very young, he can see that now. Not much more than a child. 'We wished to observe their behaviour by the light of the dark lantern.' She holds it aloft and its glow floods her face, making caverns of her eyes where her pupils are distended by the dark. Arched eyebrows. A sweet bowed mouth. 'But so far there has been no sign of them.' She turns toward the older man. 'Perhaps our light disturbed them, Grandfather?'

He is a big man, wide-shouldered and lowering. The lantern makes a mask from thick whiskers framing heavy jowls, a solid brow, a pair of spectacles. He seems less eager to engage in conversation, not with some stinking lad on his way home from drinking, fornication, God alone knew what else. Allbones senses his hostility and decides to tease.

'Your smell, more like,' he says.

'My smell?' says the girl, her voice sharpening to a pinpoint of indignation.

'No offence, Miss,' says Allbones, swaying a little in play, 'but they can't see far, badgers can't. They's blind as bats.'

'Thank you, young man,' says Grandfather Whiskers, putting his arm about the girl's shoulders. 'That's quite enough. You'll be on your way now. Good evening.' And he stands aside, leaving the way clear. Allbones has been dismissed. Ahead lies Mossop's Field, the lane and home, but something — the lateness of the hour, the weight of rabbits in his pockets, the nearness of danger — has made him giddy. He feels reckless, a match for any man. He has youth on his side, and agility, and in his hand the open blade of a sharp bone-handled knife.

'If it's cubs you're after,' he says, 'smell or no smell, you'll not see them here. There's only a couple of young boars here. The ones the old fella couldn't get on with, like.'

The girl looks up at him, all offence forgotten.

'Is that so?' she says. There's a slight lilt to her voice, along with the accents of privilege, a hint of up and down that suggests she might not be from these parts. Grandfather Whiskers is unremarkable, just one of the tribe of landowner, churchman, judge whose presence is as familiar as a tree or a wall, but whose customs are as foreign to Allbones and his kind as the customs of some South Sea Islander. They may share the same air, travel the same roads, inhabit the same landscape, but it is as though Allbones belongs to one species — a small species favouring the undergrowth, like moles or frogs or little disregarded birds — while Whiskers and his like belong to another: bigger animals whose scent is laid over wider territories. The girl is all attention now; she is looking up at Allbones and he is on home ground.

'The cubs is over there,' he says, pointing toward the deeper, darker woods. 'Under the pine where the bank's down and the ground's soft for diggin'. Boar and sows moved a month 'n' more since, when the stream backed up and flooded. They can't stand it wet in the sett, not when they're kindlin'.'

'So we've been waiting outside the wrong entrance!' The girl's disappointment is evident. 'All this time stationed here, Grandfather, while the cubs have been elsewhere!'

'There's four o' them,' Allbones adds helpfully. (He cannot resist it: a featherweight punch at the older man's pompous certainty.) 'Leastways, there was four o' them last week.' But the blow lands wide, for Whiskers, it seems, has not been paying attention, not to the exact whereabouts of badger cubs at any rate.

'So you make a habit of nightly excursions to these woods?' he says, and his voice is thoughtful and ever so slightly threatening.

Ah, thinks Allbones. Time to beat a retreat. He may have won the skirmish, but the battles always go to the men in the thick overcoats with the flourishing whiskers. All the guns are lined up on their side and while it may be amusing for a moment to prick them, they can strike back with the full force of the law and the rules they have written to suit themselves. One lazy cuff and this old man could finish Allbones for ever, consign him to four damp walls and a kind of creeping death, for Allbones knows he could not bear confinement, no matter how short the sentence. The very thought of prison brings him out in a sweat of sheer terror. No green leaf, no sky, no skitter of rabbits on a dark night. Just the slow tick of justice and the rattle of heavy keys.

He must be careful now. He answers lightly, though his hands are clammy. 'I wouldn't say nightly, sir,' he says. 'Not exactly. There's many use this path when walking from Ledney to the Bottom End. It's a deal shorter than the way by road.'

Whiskers is surveying him uncomfortably closely, from beneath the shadow cast by the peak of his Norfolk cap.

'Is that so?' he says. 'Shorter, eh?'

'Yes, sir,' says Allbones, and he sways a little, hiccups discreetly for added effect. The King's Arms. Spirits on the breath. The stagger home of the habitual drunkard, the ne'er-do-well.

'And what,' says Whiskers, his dignity fully recovered and all authority, 'might be your name, young man?'

Allbones makes a rapid reckoning. What are the chances of detection, should he lie? He has never laid eyes on this man before. A stranger here, a visitor perhaps, up for a few weeks from Cambridge or London or some other unimaginably distant place. A man whose life is lived elsewhere, importantly, doing important things. While he, Allbones, is next to invisible. One of those figures passed on the road, pressed against the hedgerow as the carriage dashes by, the horses flinging up a fine shower of gravel. A non-entity, a person of no consequence. So, what are the chances of detection? None.

'Metcalfe,' he says. 'Fowler Metcalfe.'

There: that will fix the fat bastard for the theft of Pompey, for Allbones knows his white hob is among Fowler's mess, concealed somewhere in the rickety tenement of boxes and cages in the outhouse where Fowler keeps his stock. The white hob is caged and already breeding a whole generation of lean and precious albinos for Fowler Metcalfe. To use his name is a small act of vengeance. But whatever pleasure it gives, must be short. So far Pinky has lain quiet and the rabbits have oozed and stiffened in his coat pockets and their scent has been obscured by badger musk, but his luck could yet run out. The girl seems innocent enough, all eagerness to see her cubs, but he has irritated the older man and that is never wise. He nods in the direction of the pine.

'You'll find 'em over there, Miss,' he says. 'Mebbe ten yards off.' And he attempts to edge past. But the girl reaches out her gloved hand and stops him, touching his arm.

'Thank you for your directions, Mr Metcalfe,' she says. 'You've been most kind.'

The path lies ahead, winding between the trees, then emerging into starlight between borders of nettle and Queen Anne's lace, and beyond is the field, the muddy lane, home and safety. All that holds him back is this small hand.

'Not at all, Miss,' he says. 'I hope you sees 'em. They're comical when they're at their play.'

The girl is standing close. He can look down into her face, which is raised toward him, white as a daisy. Her eyes glisten, her mouth is a pink bow, the scent of violets is overpowering. She seems in no hurry to release him. She seems in fact to be examining him too, taking in the detail of this strange young man who has stumbled upon them in the dark wood.

'We have been most fortunate to meet you this evening,' she says. 'Have we not, Grandfather?' Her face is all sweet innocence, but there is something prickling beneath the skin of the words. She is teasing, kitten-claw words intended not to flatter Allbones but to irritate the heavy-set man who glowers at her shoulder. 'We wanted so much to conduct a scientific observation, and I was quite desolate when all our efforts seemed to be for nothing. But now we have met you and received direction from a true expert.'

Allbones shuffles with discomfort. Her hand has him in a delicate vice. Now, young miss, he wants to say, don't prick your grandfather too close, or you'll have me in court.

'I'm no expert,' he says abruptly, and moves aside. 'Anyone from round here could have told you the same.' He takes a first determined step away down the star-dappled path. 'Night, sir. Night, miss.'

He walks away quickly, her 'Good night, Mr Metcalfe,'

floating into the gap that opens at his back as he forces himself not to break into a run toward the field with its incurious cows, its sweet, uncritical grass, its comfortable path beating a diagonal toward the lane and freedom.

Mary Anne stirs as he opens the door, though he is careful with the latch. She slips from the palliasse she shares with the littl'uns, leaving them in their usual tangle of arms and legs, to come and sit on the narrow stairs, hair touselled and her arms clasped about her skinny body in its thin shift.

'What did you get?' she asks.

For her benefit, Allbones puts on a play. First Pinky is drawn forth and dropped, still slumbering, back into the barrel among her siblings, where she wriggles once, twice and disappears from view into dry straw. He shakes his head sadly, draws down his mouth all the while.

'Naught,' he says. 'All laid up and no budgin' 'em.'

Mary Anne's face sags with disappointment, but 'Ah well, never mind,' she says. 'There'll be other nights.' Her feet are stone-bruised and pitted with chilblains. 'You'll be froze. I'll make you a cup of tea.' She finds the poker and stirs at the embers on the fire.

Allbones can tease no longer.

'Naught but this,' he says. And he reaches deep into the inner pocket of his coat and draws forth the doe. He drops her on the table where she lies, forepaws clasped in frozen entreaty, belly swollen with its cargo of young all still and drowned now in the watery sac.

Mary Anne's feet begin to jig around the table. 'You bawcock!' she says. 'You bessy!'

'And this,' says Allbones as the big buck joins the doe.

Then half a dozen young does, plump and tender, and a couple of bucks, until the table is covered with matted fur and glazed eyes and dry blood and the smell of damp earth fills the little room.

Mary Anne strokes the doe's soft white belly fur. 'Oh my . . .' she says. A sigh of the deepest satisfaction. By now the littl'uns have woken too, their noses twitching as the new smells break into their dreams, and here they come to gather around the table as Allbones settles to skinning and gutting, squabbling over who should get the tails for toys and being hushed — *shhh shhh* — or Mother Mossop will hear and come poking her long nose into their business.

Mary Anne helps. She has always been a capable girl: left home at ten, like all the girls in Ledney. But when Mrs Allbones took up her appointed place beneath the wild garlic outside St Peter's wall, she came home. She gave up her good position with a baker's family in Brinkton to take care of her brothers and sisters. She fetches another knife and sets to work, cutting neatly around each rabbit's ears, then drawing off the pelt as if she were drawing the vest from a squally baby. They work fast, either side of the table, until the night's takings are all bare and pink and the guts have been tipped into the barrel for the ferrets to squeal over.

'And here you are,' says Allbones to the littl'uns as he draws forth the doe's seething womb. He tips the kits onto the table: six of them, each the size of his thumb and on the verge of birth. 'One each and no arguing.' Mary Anne sets the pan on the fire and fries them up and they sizzle and spit and the room becomes suffused with the delicious smell of cooked meat and when they're done they each take their morsel, crisp and hot, and 'Ooh!' they say as their fingers are wonderfully, greasily burned, and 'Aaah!' as they snap the tiny bones in their sharp teeth and gnaw off every scrap. Then Mary Anne adds the quartered doe to the hookpot that has known only a thin gruel of turnip and potato for weeks past, and the littl'uns go back to their bed, where they curl once more to sleep, clutching a rabbit's velvety ear or the fluffy ball of a rabbit's scut against their sticky cheeks. And in their sleep they make tiny sucking noises, dreaming of meat and the promise of more in the morning.

Allbones goes out into the yard when they have settled and he has cleaned knife and board and hung all his nets to dry, for the web rots quickly if left wet and tangled. The sky is growing pale in the east and the stars are cartwheeling off across the horizon. He stands by the wall and pisses long and luxuriously, his urine smelling already of meat among the dead-nettle. Somewhere out there, Whiskers and his charge will have finished their observations, whatever they might be, and trailed home to fine sheets and soft mattresses. Somewhere out there, the badgers are waddling home to sleep on the dry grass they have dragged into nests in the sett. Somewhere out there, beyond Ledney Wood, beyond both the Ledneys, Upper and Lower, beyond Brinkton and Tolby, there's a whole wide world. But right now, pissing on the wall with Mother Mossop's Tamworth snoring in its pen a few yards away and his own brothers and sisters snug beneath their single blanket, sticky and satisfied, Walter Allbones is certain that this small corner of the world contains happiness enough.

2.

Your object is to kill them as quickly and
painlessly as possible, without injuring the
plumage. This is to be accomplished with all
small birds by suffocation . . . Squeeze the bird
tightly across the chest, under the wings, thumb
on one side, middle finger on the other,
forefinger pressed in the hollow at the foot of
the neck between the forks of the merrythought
. . . the system relaxes with a painful shiver,
light fades from the eyes and the lids close . . .
it will make you wince the first few times; you
had better hold the poor creature behind you.
J.E. Coues, *Handbook of Field and General Ornithology*,
Macmillan and Co., London, 1890.

Fowler had him pinned against the wall. Allbones' cheek was
buckled on dressed limestone, scraping on razor-sharp shreds
of ancient shell and coral.

'My name!' Fowler was hissing into his ear, his fat lips spitting anger. 'You used my name!'

His voice squeaked, like that of a woman outraged. It was the pitch plus the weight, the sheer furious bulk pressing at his back, that convinced Allbones that struggle would be useless: he could squirm and wriggle, he could protest and plead ignorance, but it was Fowler Metcalfe who had him in a strangling grip down there in the alleyway behind the High Street, and there was no hope. Fowler had weight on his side and righteous anger, not to mention the advantage of surprise.

Allbones had not been paying attention. He had been one of the raucous crowd gathered around the rat pit behind the King's Arms, where a sandy slut from over Tolby way was taking on the biggest rat anyone had ever seen, a giant buck the size of a terrier that the publican had trapped himself in his own cellar. Its appearance had caused some consternation, but the money was on the slut. She was reputed to have killed sixty-three in the allotted three minutes at Tolby, a local record.

One minute, start to finish, maybe less. That was the general opinion.

'He's a big bugger,' said the publican, 'but you know what they say: big don't always count. It's experience, pure and simple.'

To begin with it looked as if he might be right, for the buck showed no fight. It crouched, hackles raised and teeth bared, in the centre of the pit until the slut was entered, when it rose to an awkward lollop, circling the barricade, seeking escape. The landlord's watch was ticking. *Half a minute. One minute . . .*

'Go for him, darlin'!' the crowd yelled. 'He's yours!' Faces scarlet with beer and laughter and the big buck waddling about, tail whipping in a frenzy and screaming for succour, with the slut dancing after. Allbones had sized her up in an instant and known she would be a disappointment. Her owner was telling anyone who'd listen that she was sharp, she was a goer, but Allbones had never trusted sandies: quitters, in his experience. He had his money on the buck and four minutes to the kill. Maybe she'd take even longer. Maybe she'd fail alto-gether.

A minute and a half. Two minutes . . .

The crowd, seeing its wages go for nothing, was becoming furious.

'Take him! Take him!' they yelled, and the more they yelled the more the buck rat scrabbled for cover, making little dashes at the sheer walls, flinging himself toward the rim, flailing in an effort to find a grip. Allbones held on to his betting slip, counting the seconds. *Two and a half.* The slut had not even engaged. Not a scratch on that fat rump. *Three minutes.* 'Acch!' said a man beside Allbones, screwing up his slip in disgust before forcing his way back through the crowd. 'Useless craitur!'

She killed at four minutes precisely, suddenly remem-bering what it was she was there for and darting for the neck. The buck put up a feeble resistance, exhausted by his efforts to escape. Sides heaving, he managed one final piercing squeal as she cut the jugular. Blood arced into sawdust, the buck shud-dered and fell where he stood, and Allbones went to collect his winnings. Two pound, four shillings and threepence. On a single bet. The publican counted shillings and pennies into his hand with reluctant deliberation.

'You're in luck today,' he said. 'A drink to celebrate?' Pay out at the ring, take back at the bar.

But Allbones had other intentions. He pocketed the coins, feeling their comfortable weight in his trouser pocket and the Queen's profile smooth between finger and thumb. 'Later, maybe . . .' he said, and set off for the market. String for new nets, maybe new boots, some cotton print for Mary Anne to make a new dress. The one she had been given when she left her place was evidently ugly and quite out of the fashion with its bustle and frills — not that Allbones would have known. And marmady for the littl'uns . . .

Caught up in the fantasy of spending, he had not noticed Fowler. He had not seen him among the crowd at the pit, but suddenly, midway down the hill, he was grabbed from behind and bundled in a fierce headlock sideways into the alley between the High Street and the marketplace, where dogs rooted among rotting cabbages, discarded boxes and the general detritus of market day, along with the piss and the brown coils dropped by its attendees. Face up against the wall, arms pinned to his sides, a fat hand at his neck squeezing, squeezing the breath from him like a woman wringing water from a rag. He'd kicked and struggled, trying for the balls, the eye socket, anywhere he could reach, thinking of course that it was the money his assailant was after: some bastard from the rat pit had seen him pocket his winnings and had come for his share. Then the face pressed close to his neck and, in a gust of warm soupy breath, 'My name!' said Fowler Metcalfe.

He shook Allbones. A bulldog with a relentless grip.

'It were you, weren't it?'

Allbones could hear his own blood thumping and the whistle of air fighting its way through a constricted passage. Fowler's face, red and dewlapped, was pressed against his own and there was no option but full confession. Allbones had seen him often enough in one of his rages, breaking bones like twigs and blackening eyes. He'd seen him hold down a lad from Tolby in a water trough until the lad stopped kicking his shabby boots in the air, and it took four of them to intervene and drag Fowler off before he had a corpse in his furious grasp. He was peaceable enough in the normal way of things, a slow-moving lump of a lad whose ma had darted about feeding her only son like some reed warbler with its fat cuckoo.

He was indeed a foundling, for she had come upon him, a fallen chick, under a hazel in Ledney Wood, sticky with blood and creamy afterbirth and wrapped in a stained petticoat. He had been crying lustily, squiffy eyes trying to focus on the blur of green leaf overhead and pink mouth gaping. She had laid aside her basket (she was gathering ink caps, the basket full of shaggy purple). 'Uppsy-daisy, my lad,' she had said, having drawn aside the petticoat to discover the child's sex, birth-swollen to a cluster of ripe plums. Then she carried him home, where she named him for the man she would have married but for too many verses of the Ledney Carol, and fed him on milk from her nannygoat. The baby sucked hard at a rag twisted and dipped in a red clay bowl. He thrived, growing big and strong as the years passed, on a diet rich in cheese and cream and butter, though his eyes stayed squiffy and he was soft and tidy, as such lads often are, raised alone by old women.

She fought for him. Whenever the other children trailed after him singsonging 'Fatty Fowler!' or 'Bogie eyes!' she would emerge, waving a stick and screeching like any bird whose young is threatened. Tiny and fierce, she laid about, batting arms and legs at random with the length of stout hawthorn she kept behind the door for just this purpose, until her son's tormentors scattered. In time, he took care of them himself. Flourishing on the nutriment the other children of the Bottom End mostly lacked, he grew taller than them, a bulldog pup in a starched collar and heavy nailed boots. The children became more wary. When he was in a rage, his round face flushing, his voice squeaking dangerously, his squiffy eyes set in a dead hard stare, it was unwise to oppose him. He went where he pleased, he took what he pleased, and no one dared defy him. The children learned to be compliant.

And now he is full grown. His hair has thinned prematurely so that his head bursts from the collar like a naked fist and he has his hand around Allbones' throat and there's nothing Allbones can do but nod and admit that yes, it was him, since strangulation is an imminent possibility.

'Aaar!' he says, chest bursting, toes dangling several inches from the ground. Fowler, his eyes red-rimmed in deep creases of flesh like a couple of buttons stitched onto crimson velvet, gives him a little shake.

'Wha' for?' he says.

Allbones can manage only a constricted shrug as the day goes dark and stars explode behind his eyes. He could mention the hob, of course, but it would have little effect. Fowler would simply deny all knowledge, though his bogie eyes would be swivelling in all directions, the way they always do when he's lying. Fowler has always relied on strength. Lying has not been a skill he has needed to perfect.

'Bastard,' says Fowler. 'You gone and got me impilcated.'

'Implicated?' says Allbones. 'How's that then?'

Fowler shifts his weight.

'Got a message, din' I? Kid came this mornin' with a letter,' he says. 'I been "invited" up to the big house.' A knee solid as a mallet presses against Allbones' spine, threatening to snap it like so much kindling. Allbones is supple, but not supple enough for this. He feels bone buckle and cartilage stretch to tearing. 'Seems there's some new lot up there, an' they wants to meet me.'

'Dunno what you're talkin' about,' says Allbones.

'Wants my assistance, doesn' he?' says Fowler. 'Yer. This gentleman — Pitford's his name — wants me to come up to the big house so he can "call on my assistance followin' our conversation in Ledney Wood las' Friday night". Bastard.' Something quite definitely stretches and snaps somewhere in the region of Allbones' lower back.

'And my ma,' says Fowler, 'she's convinced I'm in trouble, I'm goin' to be charged or somethin', an' she's cryin' and carryin' on, she's all upset, an' I don't like my ma upset. An' the whole problem is, of course, that I don' know about any conversation an' I wasn' anywhere near Ledney Wood las' Friday. Was I?'

Allbones can only grunt.

'But,' says Fowler, fist tightening, 'it din' take a whole lot of workin' out to think who might've been up in Ledney Wood las' Friday and who might, at a squeeze, have used my name. Bastard!' The stars begin to pop once more. 'It were you, weren' it?'

Allbones nods and manages a despairing whiffle that might have been understood as a yes.

'I knew it!' says Fowler. His breath is a stale bouquet of butter, onions, cutlets and ale. 'So, what did you two talk about, then, you and this gentleman?'

'Nothing,' gasps Allbones, his face scraping to bloody mincemeat. Fowler's fist tightens dangerously. 'Badgers! We talked about badgers!'

'Oh yer?' says Fowler, and his voice is heavy with menace.

'Yer!' says Allbones. 'Badgers! They was out in the wood, doin' observations of badgers.' Even to his ear it does not sound particularly convincing.

'They?' says Fowler.

'There was a girl,' says Allbones.

'Oh yer?' says Fowler, sounding more interested.

'Yer,' says Allbones, pressing his advantage. 'Just a kid. Thirteen, fourteen maybe. They was observin' that set up by the old road.'

' "Observin"!' says Fowler. 'That's a new word for it.'

'Nothin' like that,' says Allbones. 'This Pitford's her grandfather. They was lookin' for cubs.' He is chattering now, seeking diversion, anything that might loosen that hand at his throat. He can hear people passing by only a few yards away on the High Street, their boots tapping on paving stones, but Fowler's great bulk blocks all escape. 'The girl wanted to see them, but they was lookin' in the wrong place. They din' know they'd moved. After the floodin', you know? They moved to that new sett . . .'

Fowler is not really interested. Badgers are dull, plodding sport, in his opinion, though he's dug a few in his time. Give him a rat any day over a badger. A female rat with a nest to defend that'll fight to the death. Or a wild cat. He shifts his weight in a leisurely fashion and twists Allbones' arm against his back in a casual lock. Clavicle and scapula creak ominously.

'So,' he says, 'why does this gentleman want to see you again?'

'Not me,' says Allbones. 'You. Fowler Metcalfe.'

'Not likely,' says Fowler as he twists Allbones' arm so that it threatens to burst from its socket. 'You got into this, you get out.'

'I'm not goin' up to the big house,' says Allbones.

'Oh yes you are,' says Fowler. And it seems as if Allbones will indeed be going, minus one arm. 'You don' have a choice. This Mr Pitford wants to see the individual he met las' Friday night. He has somethin' to discuss with him, which "could be to their mutual benefit". Two o'clock Tuesday. All right?'

'What's he mean?' says Allbones. '"Mutual benefit"?'

'Dunno,' says Fowler. 'Maybe he wants to discuss badgers.' He enjoys his little joke. 'Yer! Badgers! Or maybe he wants to have a little chat about what you might have had in your pockets up there in Ledney Wood. But I don't care much what he wants to talk about, because it's not goin' to be me he's talkin' to, is it? It's you. Got it?'

'Got it,' says Allbones, arm furled flat as a wing against his backbone. 'Yer, I got it.'

'You go up there, you clear up any misunderstandin', you clear my name,' says Fowler. 'Tuesday. Two o'clock. Say it!'

'Tuesday. Two o'clock,' says Allbones.

'On the dot,' says Fowler.

'On the dot,' says Allbones.

And at last Fowler releases him. Allbones straightens cautiously, feeling bone and muscle clip back into their customary configuration.

'Right,' says Fowler, all business now, the fury subsiding as rapidly as it had risen. 'Here's your invitation, Cinderella. Don' lose it.' He tucks a piece of cream notepaper into the top pocket of Allbones' jacket and picks up his own hat from where it has fallen during the scuffle. 'An' don' you ever use my name again. A good name is rather to be chosen than great riches an' don' you fuckin' forget it.' He has always been a great one for the quotations. He rubs his hat brim clean and jams it down on his naked skull, then straightens coat and collar and walks off up the alley, moving with the insouciant delicacy of the fat man bouncing along on the very tips of his toes. His pink lips pucker as he turns the corner. 'He swings through the air . . .' he whistles, stepping out onto the busy street. 'That daring young man on the . . .' He has gone.

And that was how Walter Allbones found himself at two o'clock on a sunny afternoon in May ringing the bell at a kitchen door to which he had been directed by a gardener carrying a tray of seedling lobelias.

'Round there,' he'd said, gesturing with a bristled chin and a fine disdain for this scrawny youth, hair slicked flat as a newborn pup's, neck and hands scrubbed, coat brushed and boots polished with soot and candlegrease to a fine gleam while the littl'uns had stood around, open-mouthed at the glamour of their brother's clean clothes and regal invitation.

The gardener was less impressed. Not much older than Allbones but in possession of a new position, regular pay and lodging, he scarcely paused in his purposeful stride toward the south lawn where they were to lay out carpet beds in patterns of crimson (petunias), silver (lamb's ear) and blue (lobelias), two hundred of each and rain threatening.

'Trade's round back,' he said, when Allbones said he'd been sent for, he had a letter, presenting it as proof. 'This path's House only. The gate's over there, past them sequoias.' He seemed to mean some spindly trees gathered in a group on the far side of an expanse of velvety lawn.

Allbones crunched off miserably from the wrong path and onto the right path, trying to ignore the lads at work clipping and digging, and the way they grinned at one another as he passed. His back scalded under his ill-fitting jacket and the hairs at the base of his neck bristled as any creature's will when in hostile territory. Past the spindly sapling trees and others that bore no resemblance to the trees he knew — oak, ash, yew — but had a few leaves like little fans, or clusters of blue needles, or trunks patchworked in crimson, cream and brown. Trees which, though young, required tying down with stout stakes and wire as if they were so flighty, so highly bred, that they might at any moment take off back to where they belonged. Silver labels had been tacked to their skinny trunks. He passed close enough to make out words but they made no sense to him: a flock of trees had landed on an English lawn wearing badges and were as out of place and uncomfortable here as Allbones himself.

The house stood on his left, built of golden stone and set square to the south. One wall, however, had been recently reconstructed and burst into a bubble of curving metal and scales of shimmering glass. Within its frail shelter, Allbones could make out the forms of plants as odd as those that had invaded the lawn: giant ferns, bigger by far than the ferns of Ledney Wood, while from beyond the house came those shrieks and whoops, the strange calls that had puzzled him for weeks past. They belonged to this place where trees had to be tethered like wild beasts and a man could easily take the wrong path.

At last he was at the gate and passing with relief into a more familiar place where buildings stored ordinary things like garden forks and wheelbarrows, saw-benches and bales of straw. Back here, the house had stopped trying to impress and was plain and unadorned. There was a door in a wall: an ordinary door with a reassuring bucket by the step and a bench where someone had set down some plain English carrots and a comfortable cabbage. A cat sat in a patch of sunlight licking its fur and the smells emanating from an open window were of fried onions and seared beef, and a fruit cake when it is browned and ready to take from the oven. He pressed the bell.

'Well?' said a brisk little cook like a roll of unproven dough in a floury pinafore. Allbones stood on the bottom step, longing for escape, to run as fast as he could move for the back gate and the right path, which would take him back to the Bottom End. Awkwardly he removed his hat, a broken bowler he had found one morning rolling happily along the road all by itself in a westerly gale as if it were off on a spree. It sat a little large on Allbones' pin head, perching upon his ears, which folded beneath the brim like small pink brackets. He clutched it now in sticky fingers.

'I'm sent for,' he said.

'Sent for?' sniffed the cook. 'Who sent for you?' She could pick a shifty one at fifty paces and this was a shifty one, no doubt about it. This one was a master of shiftiness, with his slick hair and boots so scuffed no polish could conceal it. He'd be off with whatever he could lay his paws on. He seemed unable to speak up but licked his shifty lips and handed over a letter, crumpled and smudged with sweat.

'Well . . .' she said, scanning it briefly. 'Well, well . . . so it's Mr Pitford himself who wants to see you. Hmmm . . .' She looked him over once more, clearly at a loss to explain the strange impulses of her betters, then called over one shoulder, 'Colin!' Not taking her eyes off him for one second.

A gangly youth like a seedling left too long under a winter cloche emerged from a room down the long corridor behind. He wore blue striped apron; in one hand he held a towel, in the other a tin of silver polish.

'Here,' said the cook, 'you leave them forks and escort . . .' — she gave the word a most particular emphasis — 'this . . .' — a pause as she searched for the right word — 'person', she settled for at last — 'upstairs. I'll ring for Mr Weavers to meet you at the door.'

She stood aside, wiping her hands on her pinafore front as Allbones stepped up, wishing desperately for the first time in his life that he was a praying man. A praying man with direct access to the Almighty who might, given sufficient prompting, fashion an earthquake or a deluge of fiery rain, anything at all that guaranteed release. He held out his hand, from which repeated scrubbing had been unable to dislodge a whole tiny landscape of dirty crevices.

'What now?' said the cook disagreeably. There was a cake to ice for tea, a beef Wellington to prepare for dinner and a new girl who was all thumbs and no idea at all about the difference between to chop and to julienne.

'My letter?' said Allbones.

'Oh,' said the cook, and handed it over carelessly. From down the corridor in the direction of the kitchen there came the sudden noisy clatter of something falling onto a flagged floor to the accompaniment of raised voices. 'What now?' she said again and waddled off at a rapid jog-trot, haunches rolling beneath her full skirt, like a heifer returning to its stall.

Colin removed his apron in silence and hung it carefully behind the silver-room door before making an elaborate show of locking the door and placing the key in his vest pocket. He

47

smoothed his hair like a girl who has glimpsed herself in a shop window, then walked off down the corridor, and Allbones had no choice but to follow.

There was a dimly lit warren of rooms down here: walls of sour-cream plaster opened onto scullery, pot room, fruit store, linen closet. Colin looked to neither left nor right but marched ahead with an easy proprietorial stride while Allbones scurried behind, glancing in at white plates stacked upon a rack; a side of beef hung from a hook with legs spread, marbled white and bloody red; gleaming copper; shadowy shelves laid with orderly ranks of apples and pears. His boots clicked on bare boards. Colin turned left, then right, opened a glass door onto another corridor. Unguided, Allbones would have been lost in an instant. He could feel the clutch of claustrophobia at his throat, down here so far from the open air and the sky, and he had to force himself to breathe steadily, in and out, in and out, trapped in a maze and all because of the white hob and that thieving bastard Fowler Metcalfe.

His sweating hands clenched to fists. Ahead, Colin turned a corner and set off up a short flight of steps leading to a door covered in soft green, as if timber had decided to sprout a luxuriant coat of moss, and suddenly they were emerging into blinding light. Allbones took a moment to focus on a hexagonal hall tiled in a dizzying pattern of black and white. Doors opened at every angle, tall and narrow and crowned with men's heads, white and eyeless and draped, where the shoulders had been severed, with a twist of plaster linen. Glass cabinets occupied the walls between each set of doors, and in each cabinet were creatures Allbones at first presumed to be living, for they were perched upon branches or peering from tangled leaves, all bright eyes and frisky tails as if interrupted in their play by the unexpected arrival of two young men breaking from below ground like a couple of moles, blinking into daylight. A sturdy man in sober black came tittupping across the marble floor on highly polished shoes.

'Visitor for Mr Pitford, Mr Weavers,' said Colin languidly, as if handing over a parcel of no particular importance. 'He's got a letter. Two o'clock.' And as he said it the clock above one of the doors sounded in sombre endorsement. Two o'clock. On the dot. While from behind other doors and from overhead where a flight of stairs curved away into the unknown came other tinklings and chimings. Two o'clock, on the dot.

'Thank you, Colin,' said Mr Weavers and Colin, relieved of his charge, slid back behind the baize door and into silence. Mr Weavers held out his hand and for a second Allbones wondered if he meant to shake hands. Was that what such grand people did in such grand places? Mr Weavers clicked his fingers impatiently. 'The letter,' he said. 'The letter!' Flushing, Allbones handed it over: a damp scrap of paper which Mr Weavers held by its very edge, as if it might carry some nameless and deadly disease. He scanned it, raising his eyebrows in a dumbshow of disapproval.

'Right, you,' he said, setting off across the vestibule to knock discreetly at one of the narrow doors where he stood for a second, head inclined to polished oak, listening to the heart beating within. He turned the handle.

'Mr Metcalfe,' he said, all formality, 'sir.' The pause was minuscule, but sufficient to permit just a whiff of disapproval at his employer's choice of guest.

'Thank you, Weavers,' said a voice: preoccupied, a little distant, but still recognisably the voice from Ledney Wood.

Weavers turned to go and as he passed Allbones in the

doorway he said, 'You behave yourself, you hear?' but so quickly, so quietly, with no obvious movement of the lips that Allbones could not be quite sure he had heard correctly. The door clicked to behind his stately back.

Allbones found himself marooned on a crimson carpet woven with flowers and tendrils of leaf in a long, rectangular room. A fire burned in the grate and sunlight fell full through tall windows, casting brilliant rectangles over carpet and polished floor and a massive central desk where Whiskers — Mr Pitford — sat at work. By day he was revealed as a man of solid proportions, with an exuberant beard and a broad pale face. His hair was grey sprinkled with traces of an earlier black and sprang from a skull set heavily on a thick neck and broad shoulders. He sat at his desk writing steadily. No 'Good afternoon', no 'How d'you do', no sign of noticing that anyone had entered the room at all, least of all a gawky young man clutching a broken-brimmed bowler hat. Pen nearly invisible between beefy fingers he wrote, dipping into a silver inkwell and from time to time pausing to gaze vacantly at a spot a foot or two above Allbones' bare head.

'Ahh,' he said then. And 'Hmmm . . .'

And sometimes he sighed deeply, as if weighed down by matters of great moment. When he looked up, his eyes were hooded and colourless behind steel-rimmed glasses that had slid to the end of his nose and lodged against its bulbous tip. His moustache bore the ochre stains of the habitual tobacco smoker. His jacket was country tweed the colour of autumn leaves and dry bracken, and beneath the desk his shoes were visible, polished to a brilliant chestnut sheen. All this Allbones had ample time to observe as he waited upon the carpet, feet trapped by a tangle of woven flower and vine.

On the wall between the windows stood shelves where books formed rows of buff and red and green tooled with gold, and glass-fronted cabinets like the ones he had glimpsed in the vestibule. In the cabinet immediately to his left a couple of birds with big flat orange paddling feet and crests brushed erect stood upon a rock. One held in its beak a fish, so brilliantly enamelled it might have been plucked fresh from the waves painted about their feet. The cabinet walls had been painted with a landscape of vertiginous cliffs and foaming seas. Allbones had been to the sea once, as a child on a Sunday School outing. The day had been grey and the sea had spread flat as a turnip field ploughed by a chill wind. The vast, desolate space had frightened him terribly, though it had been supposed to be a treat, with games on the sand and a toffee to suck. The sea in the cabinet was brilliant blue, streaked with purple and green.

The cabinet to his right contained an assembly of lizards far larger than any lizard Allbones had ever seen in his life. A foot and more in length, they sunned themselves upon an arrangement of stones or, like the dragons in some children's tale, raised clawed heraldic feet, frozen in the act of fighting. Their mouths gaped, revealing small sharp teeth and startlingly red tongues. They snarled at one another and at whoever might be peering in at them behind the glass. Beyond that cabinet stood another where some round brown birds pecked desultorily at some scraps of dry autumnal woodland while above their heads two pigeons with feathers of luminous bluegreen and white vests perched feasting on branches of hawthorn. Cabinet after cabinet, each bearing its little drama of birds and animals in their painted kingdom, and between them shelves bearing strange instruments of brass and polished wood, and banks of narrow drawers, and books books books in their buff and red and green.

All this Allbones saw from his vantage point upon the flowery rug.

In the furthest corner of the room, behind the blockade formed by Pitford's desk, stood a table. A bird stood upon it, a tall brown bird with its beak raised toward the ceiling amid an artful arrangement of bulrushes. On the table lay pens and brushes, a palette covered in dabs of brown and ochre and green, a jar of muddy water, a rag or two, around a small raised dais to which a sheet of creamy parchment had been pinned. Allbones was too distant to make out any image upon the paper but he could see a chair before the table, pushed aside as if its occupant had just recently leapt up and left the room.

Allbones saw it all: the fire in the grate, the dragons fighting, the fish shining as if it were alive. He could smell paint and ink and coal burning and polished wood and clean linen and the dry whiff of vellum and paper and tobacco and, threaded through all this, the pale scent of violets. He stood upon the rug with his hat in his sweaty hands, waiting for this discussion, whatever that might entail. Accusation, no doubt. To be followed by denial on his part, and furious improvisation, to be followed by the submission of proof, some detail he had overlooked, to be followed inevitably by the summoning of the law, the arrival of the constable from Brinkton with baton and cuffs, to be followed by imprisonment, his sisters and brothers on the parish, failure and loss . . .

'Hmmm . . .' said Pitford, laying his pen aside and leaning back with a satisfied air. He looked up and seemed startled. Who was this young man who had arrived somehow upon the

Bokhara, and who clearly awaited his attention?

'Ah . . . Metcalfe.' The name was recalled with some effort. 'Our expert in the habits of the badger!'

'I wouldn't say that, sir,' said Allbones. And this, of course, was the moment when he should have corrected the misunderstanding. He should have said that his name was not Metcalfe but Allbones, but that would have required explanation, it would have involved embarrassment and awkwardness and the man behind the desk was not the startled individual caught unawares out in the woods on a dark night, but a man at his ease in his own room. Allbones said nothing more, and the moment for explanation slid past.

'It was you we met the other night, was it not?' said Pitford. 'In Ledney Wood?'

'I believe so, sir,' said Allbones miserably. Here it came: the 'discussion'.

'Who directed us toward the principal sett?' said Pitford.

'Just trying to help, sir,' said Allbones. 'The young lady seemed keen to see the cubs.'

'Indeed she was,' said Pitford. 'And, thanks to you, our expedition was crowned with success. We found them under the pine.'

'Glad to hear it, sir,' said Allbones.

'So,' said Pitford, flexing fingers cramped from writing. 'You know this area well, it seems?'

Allbones was careful. 'A little, sir,' he said.

'Come now, Metcalfe,' said the older man. 'I'd say you know it like the back of your hand. I would say that you are, after your own fashion, quite the natural scientist.'

'I don't think so, sir,' said Allbones. What was the man talking about?

Pitford leaned back in his chair, fingers arched. 'You take note of the habits of badgers,' he said. 'You are intrigued by the creatures here on display.'

Allbones flushed. He had thought himself unobserved.

'I never seen anything quite like 'em before,' he said. 'Them lizards an' that.'

Pitford smiled. 'Quite so,' he said. 'And these?' He gestured toward the cabinet where the brown birds pecked among dry oak leaves. 'What do you make of those?'

'Quail, sir,' said Allbones. 'Leastways, they have the look of a quail, but darker than quail from round these parts, and more stocky, like.'

'And these?' Pitford pointed to the birds feasting on berries.

'Pigeons,' said Allbones. 'But I never seen pigeons that size before, nor with that bright colour.'

Pitford was pleased. 'A natural scientist, Metcalfe,' he said. 'Untrained, of course, but with the correct disposition.' He took a pipe from the rack. 'Which brings me to the reason for this interview.'

He tapped the bowl smartly upon a silver ashtray, then set to work removing shreds of blackened tobacco with a small silver pick.

'You are a young man who knows Ledney Wood and its environs in some considerable detail.'

'Maybe I am, sir,' said Allbones.

'I am sure of it,' said Pitford, squinting down the stem of his pipe. 'I have made some enquiries since our encounter last Friday evening, and I have been assured that you have the reputation of being a man with a considerable knowledge of the local fauna.'

He was at ease here, in a way he had not been out there in the dark wood. This was his territory, where the younger man was the intruder, trapped among cabinetry in which the natural splendours of the world had been captured, labelled, studied and understood. He picked burnt shreds from the pipe and dropped them one by one into the ashtray.

'Quite a reputation,' he said. 'I believe you are reputed to be expert on not just the habits of badgers, Metcalfe, but on the habits of mustelids in general.'

'Mustelids?' said Allbones.

'*Mustela erminea*,' said Pitford evenly. 'The stoat. *Mustela nivalis*. The weasel. And most particularly, *Mustela putorius*. The ferret.'

Allbones was sweating. The room felt airless. His shirt collar, washed for the occasion, had become a noose about his neck.

'Yes, ferrets,' said Pitford. He replaced the pick upon the rack. 'My source was most specific. "If it's ferrets you wish to discuss, Fowler Metcalfe is your man." You breed them, I believe?'

'One or two,' said Allbones. 'To keep the rats at bay, like. There's a terrible plague of rats round Ledney.'

For rats. Not for rabbits, and especially not for rabbits that lived within someone else's walls. But Pitford had begun to fill the pipe with fresh tobacco. His thick fingers pressed the shreds into the bowl slowly, carefully. He seemed unconcerned about the precise purpose for which Allbones' ferrets might be bred.

'Indeed,' he said. 'A plague indeed . . .'

Where was all this headed? Allbones waited miserably, mesmerised by the glint of steel-rimmed glasses, trapped in a burrow stop.

'The fact is, Metcalfe, that I could do with the assistance of a man like yourself, a man with a strong practical knowledge of this part of the country. The kind of knowledge you displayed last Friday evening.' Pipe filled, he reached for a lucifer. 'Yes . . .' he said, drawing in in little gasps. 'The knowledge — gasp — a man acquires — gasp — who spends his nights — gasp gasp — in the woods.' Smoke poured from mouth and nostrils and formed a small particular cloud above his heavy head.

Allbones' heart tripped. 'The King's Arms,' he said desperately. 'I been there all evening. You can ask the landlord. He'll confirm . . .'

But Pitford cut off his protestations. 'I am not interested in confirmation,' he said. 'Your whereabouts earlier that evening is of no concern to me whatsoever. What I am interested in is acquiring the assistance of a man with just your expertise. A discreet man, who can keep his business to himself. And I think you might be the man I am looking for.'

'Is that so, sir?' said Allbones. This discussion was not following the path he had expected but was darting about in surprising directions, like a hare sprung on an open field.

'The fact is,' said Pitford, 'I wish to acquire some ferrets.'

The cloud of tobacco smoke broke and drifted toward the window. Ferrets? This gentleman wished to acquire ferrets?

'Ferrets, or stoats, or weasels,' said Pitford. 'Whatever you can lay your hands on. I suspect that ferrets might be the simplest to find at short notice.'

Allbones was astonished. Men of Pitford's kind were not normally to be found in the mêlée behind the King's Arms.

'I gather you breed the creatures and trade in them. And

I gather your stock is reputed to be the best in the county: the sturdiest, the most vigorous. I should like to do business with you.'

The best! thought Allbones. Fowler Metcalfe's stock 'the best'? Who in their right mind would prefer Fowler's stock to Allbones', bred pale, fast and lethal over years of careful selection? Who would choose one of Fowler's sandies over one of Allbones' whites?

'There's others round here as breed 'em better,' he said. He could not help himself, torn between discretion and professional pride. 'Metcalfe's — I mean, *my* stock is sound enough, but I seen stock to outclass it, I have to admit. Walter Allbones, for instance, down Bottom End. Now, his ferrets is better'n mine. And there's many as says so.'

Pitford nodded in approval, pipe clamped and smoking fiercely.

'That is exactly the kind of thing I wanted to hear,' he said. 'The candid opinion of the expert.'

'Thank you, sir,' said Allbones.

'But I have not made the acquaintance of this Allbones,' said Pitford, 'whereas chance has introduced me to you, Metcalfe. The pre-eminent expert. You know the country, you know the breed, you know the breeders round about.'

'Perhaps I do, sir,' said Allbones.

'So,' said Pitford, 'to the matter in hand: ferrets.'

'Shouldn't be no trouble finding them this time of year,' said Allbones. 'You'll be wanting them for baiting, or for breeding?'

'Breeding,' said Pitford.

'So you'll be wanting a hob,' said Allbones. 'And a few sluts? Whites or sandies?'

They had odd tastes, the rich. You'd think they would stick to their horses, their Grand Nationals and their view halloo after foxes, rather than bothering with such small stuff as ferrets, rabbits and rats and a few bob at the pit.

'The colour is immaterial,' said Pitford. 'It's quantity I'm after.'

'How many do you want?'

'Three hundred,' said Pitford. 'Three hundred and fifty. As many as you can find.'

'Three hundred and fifty?'

'Assorted,' said Pitford. 'Ferrets, of course, and stoats, and weasels, if you can catch them. Young stock, with years of breeding in them. Easy to handle, ideally, and accustomed to confinement.'

'Three hundred and fifty?'

'We could use more, but we are limited unfortunately by the practicalities of transport.'

'Transport?' said Allbones. He seemed to have turned into one of those birds that answers another's call with its echo. What had transport to do with the case?

'These creatures are destined for great things, Mr Metcalfe,' said Pitford. 'They are to supply the nucleus of a new colony. They are to be dispatched to the other side of the world, where they will be employed as they have been employed in these islands since the days of Caesar and his legions, in the control of rabbits. For *Oryctolagus cuniculus* is proving yet again, when introduced to virgin territory devoid of any customary predators, to be a tasty but troublesome guest. As history might have warned us he would . . .'

Pitford leaned back, pipe clenched between his teeth and settled to his theme, his hands placed fingertip to fingertip, his voice taking on a grander tone as if he were addressing a whole assembly of eager students and not a single miserable youth in greasy corduroys.

'Yes indeed . . . the geographer Strabo has recorded the experience of the Gymnesiae, the inhabitants of those islands we now know as Majorca and Minorca, whose lands were stripped bare by the descendants of a single pair of rabbits, introduced there from their place of origin on the Iberian Peninsula. The very name of that peninsula suggests their breeding capacities — a litter of ten every month, as you are no doubt aware, Mr Metcalfe, following your own observations, and every kit ready to breed the minute it leaves the nest. So prolific were they that the Phoenicians, those great mariners of yore, called the land "i Shephanim" or "the coast of the rabbit". From which derives its modern name, Hispania.'

He gave the name a fine foreign flourish. Smoke curled about his head, his eyes were half closed behind the steel spectacles and focused not on Allbones but on distant centuries.

'From this single Lagomorphic Adam and Eve a vast progeny had sprung, so that the very houses of the Gymnesiae were being undermined, trees were toppling, crops were being consumed and famine threatened. Strabo is, of course, not always the most reliable of witnesses. In the same book in which he records the plague of rabbits, he describes tunny fish that feast upon acorns from oak forests flourishing beneath the waves, and the manner in which great deposits of gold and silver are drawn from the soil of the region by setting fire to the forests above, to the effect that their great heat melts the metal and every mountain exudes riches as other mountains produce springs of water. But in the matter of rabbits, those little gnawing creatures Strabo calls "leberides", we can, I believe, place some credence.'

Allbones waited patiently. What was all this about, these gyminy folk, this hisparnee? What had they to do with three hundred ferrets?

Pitford rumbled on from behind his cloud like the picture of God seated among the cherubim above the chancel arch in St Peter's Ledney.

'So great were the depredations of the rabbit that the Gymnesians were forced to send a deputation to Caesar Augustus, requesting his aid. The mighty force of the Roman army was to be unleashed against the rabbit! And, should that fail, the only alternative they could envisage was resettlement. Yes — the Gymnesians were prepared to abandon temple and hearth to the invader and move elsewhere, as the inhabitants of Abdera in Thrace had been driven from their homes by a plague of rats and frogs to resettle on the frontiers of Macedonia.'

Pitford's pipe appeared to have expired. He examined it, then tapped it upon the edge of the desk.

'History supplies the precedent, Metcalfe, and it is history, too, that teaches the solution. The "wild cats from Africa", which Strabo tells us were muzzled and turned into the burrows where they compelled the denizens to fly to the surface in their thousands, there to be dispatched by hunters. "The wild cats from Africa." Ferrets, Metcalfe! Ferrets!'

At last, thought Allbones. He was getting to the subject.

'For the mustelid, the smallest of all flesh-eating mammals, is the most savage. It must kill and consume more in proportion to its weight than the larger carnivores. A lion, for example, need kill only every four or five days, while the tiny mustelid must hunt daily. So the bloodthirsty ferret came to the aid of the Gymnesiae, as now it will lend its assistance to rescue the New Zealander from ruin!'

Pipe returned to the rack and lecture over, Pitford leaned forward and fixed Allbones with a steady stare, all business.

'Strong animals, in the full vigour of youth,' he said. 'Fit to breed and rid the land of a plague! For animals such as these, delivered in good condition by the end of the summer, I shall pay a good price.'

Allbones waited. How much?

'Four shillings a head,' said Pitford. 'What do you say to that?'

Allbones made a rapid calculation. Reading and writing he had never taken to. Words made no sense, spelled every which way. But numbers were different. They meant what they said. Three hundred and fifty ferrets at four shillings a head. Fourteen hundred shillings. Seventy pounds! In all Allbones' life of seasonal improvisation — bird-scaring, turnip-hoeing, ditch-digging, dyke-clearing, cadging odd jobs wherever he could — he had never been offered so much. Ten shillings a week, if the work was to be had. Seventy pounds!

'I'd have to buy in,' he said. 'I've only half a dozen from my own breeding.'

Four shillings a head, when they could be had for two, if it was just breeding stock he was after and not anything special — a white hob, for instance. Should he risk asking for more, or take what he had been offered?

'And it'd have to be kept quiet, like,' he said. 'Once the lads round here worked out there was a market, there's no telling what they'd ask.'

'That is exactly as I would wish it to be,' said Pitford. 'These ferrets of yours are to be part of an exchange, and in trade I find it is always best to be discreet. Let us keep our contract to ourselves: a few animals purchased here — presumably for your own use — a few purchased there — and no mention of our discussion here today.'

Allbones needed no persuasion. Discretion was a lesson he had learned long since at his mother's knee. 'Keep yoursel' to yoursel',' she'd counselled. 'No blash, no blather, no clattin' in and out of others' doors.' And she'd given him a sharp rap across the knuckles with the wooden spoon to help him remember. Allbones had been a quiet lad who customarily hung about the edges of the crowd at the King's Arms and kept a still tongue in his head.

'I'll not say a word,' he said, and Pitford could see he meant it.

'Good man,' he said. 'So — shall we say thirty within the fortnight, just to show you're up for it? A small advance . . .' He took an envelope from a drawer and laid it on the desk. 'Then payment on receipt of each consignment. Three hundred and fifty by the end of September ready for dispatch in October.'

The end of September. Four months. It would be tight. He would have to spread the net wide, taking in men with breeding stock all over the county, travel to distant pits without arousing suspicion, trap what he could. But four shillings a head! Seventy pound, near on half of it likely to be profit! He shook with the unexpected shift from trepidation and the expectation of arrest to the probability of riches. Wouldn't Fowler rage if he were to discover the exact nature of the discussion he had so strenuously avoided? Not that that sweet moment would ever occur, at least not if Allbones could avoid it.

'Delivered to the stableyard every Friday, where one of my men — Donnithorne — will pay you and attend to their housing and care.'

'I'll do my best,' said Allbones as he took up the envelope clinking with coins. How Pompey's theft had been avenged!

At that moment there was a light *tap tap* at the door behind him. A cool rush of air as it opened. The rustle of petti-coats and a muted flurry of 'Oh, excuse me! I didn't mean to disturb . . .' The scent of violets.

Pitford extended a paternal arm.

'Come in, Eugenia,' he said. 'We have completed our business, have we not, Mr Metcalfe?'

The girl was fair with hair so blonde it was almost white, gathered in a knot then left to tumble loose about her shoul-ders. At the mention of his name, she turned and held out her hand.

'Mr Metcalfe!' she said. 'Our expert!' For a second their hands touched, his scratched with broken grubby nails, hers clean and cool. 'Four cubs — and they were as you promised, enchanting. Thank you.'

As if the woods and all that dwelt within them had been his to bestow.

'Glad to hear it, Miss,' he said.

He lifted his eyes from a determined study of the carpet. Her eyes were blue, the blue you glimpse when you look up to the sky through spring leaf, and in the curve of the iris he could see his own reflection held upside down, like a man suspended in mid-air. Her skin was like eggshell, and the tracery of veins was visible on her forehead and in the curves of her neck. He could see the tiny peck of the pulse. For himself, it was as though blood and breath had ceased. She regarded him steadily, while he looked down at her in a confusion of pleasure and panic. Then the room became present once more, with its sunlit windows, its cabinets, its burning logs, and she broke away, her hand flying to her mouth.

'I came to say . . .' she said, turning to her grandfather. 'I came to tell you . . . the woodhens have arrived!'

'Already?' said Pitford, getting to his feet. 'But they were not due until tomorrow!'

'I know, I know,' said the girl. 'But nevertheless they are here. The wagon is at the aviary gate. Now — you don't wish to send them off to return another day, do you?'

'No, by George, I don't!' said Pitford, buttoning his coat and flinging open one of the tall doors leading to the terrace. Allbones thought he was to be left once again abandoned upon the crimson rug, but 'Come along, come along, Mr Metcalfe!' said the girl. 'This will be of interest to you!' And there was no option but to follow as she ran after her grandfather, hair flying, along the terrace with its urns of trees clipped to geometrical shapes, down some steps to a gravel path and through a gate in a high stone wall.

Behind the wall lay an enclosure lined with cages in various stages of completion: some half built, some finished but empty, some already occupied with fluttering, squawking, whistling — the odd cries he had heard in the distance for the past few months as he was occupied in the exercise of his profession within and without the walls of the estate. A gate in the opposite wall stood open where a wagon was drawn up. A carrier was unloading a wooden crate into the outstretched arms of a couple of men under the supervision of a fussy and particular individual in dusty travelling clothes. Pitford quickened his stride.

'Careful! Careful!' he shouted as the crate lurched and the men struggled to take its weight before lowering it gently to earth. Pitford fell to his knees before it, oblivious to mud or dung, and peered between the timbers.

'I think you'll find all as it should be, Mr Pitford,' said the traveller, a Scot by the sound of him, with evident relief. 'Four were lost in the Antarctic Ocean to a rogue wave, as I informed you by telegraph. And three succumbed for causes I could not determine. But this pair has survived — and I must say that I am glad of it, for it has been with great effort. In fact, I hope never to have to set foot on a boat again, not if it were the phoenix itself that were to be the trophy!'

Pitford stood and dusted off his trousers. 'I am profoundly grateful to you, Mr Tweedie,' he said, pumping the traveller's hand with enthusiasm. 'The world of natural study and experiment owes you and your fellows in the field its deepest thanks. So — you have brought me a pair!'

'A pair,' said the traveller. 'In breeding condition.'

'Capital!' said Pitford. He was like a child with a Christmas parcel, eager to tear open the wrappings. 'Now, let us see what we have won, despite rogue wave and disease! Over here! Over here!' The men bent to lift the crate and, since Allbones was standing by, it was natural for him to take a corner too and shuffle with it, knees buckling under its weight, following Pitford, who led the way to one of the empty cages. The floor was concrete, but deeply strewn with leaves of oak and beech around a hollow log. The rear wall had been painted like the display cabinets within the house, with a landscape: a vista of snow-capped mountains, framed by a grove of those tall fern trees.

The crate was levered open and Pitford reached in, with cautions from Mr Tweedie — 'Careful! They've a powerful beak and a most uncooperative disposition!' — and drew forth an unremarkable brown bird. It shrieked in alarm and flapped wildly, but he grasped it and held it close, examining it minutely.

'The wing, you see,' he said to himself as much as to any bystanders, 'is fully formed. But the quills, though broad, are too soft to sustain flight, while the inner secondaries . . .' he spread the wing wide like a tawny fan '. . . are no more than a loose mantle. What more perfect proof could one have of the laws of natural adaptation? In the absence of predators, the bird has no need of flight and its wings have become as redundant as a Beefeater's pikestaff: once essential for survival, now no more than ornament!'

Under this examination the bird struggled, its feathers releasing a strong odour reminiscent of mouldy straw, stale fish or maggoty meat, the stink of long confinement. It squirmed, managing to free one wing, which instantly left a gash on its captor's hand. Pitford seemed delighted with this show of independence.

'See!' he said, as blood trickled down his wrist and soaked his shirt cuff. 'Proof absolute of its correct assignation to the species *Gallirallus*!' He took firm hold of the wing and picked the feathers apart. 'There! On the joint. The spur that characterises all rails!'

He bent down and carefully released the bird into the cage, where it ran immediately to the farthest corner, tail feathers flickering. 'And there the identity is confirmed: the flirt of moorhen and coot! This is the male, is it not?' He turned to the traveller as the bird's cries roused a shrill reply from within the crate.

'I believe so,' said Tweedie over the din. 'They're not as easy as some to sex. Beak and plumage appear to be identical so far as I can tell, and there is no visible dimorphism. Size, weight, habit, call — all indistinguishable. I dissected several specimens in the field and that clears the matter conclusively, of course, but with a live pair, there is little one can do but wait for the first breeding season when the female's vent may swell and soften.'

He flushed the instant the words had left his prim mouth, glancing side on at Eugenia, but she was absorbed in watching her grandfather take the second bird from the crate. It emerged shrieking, thrashing with its muscular legs and, finally, as Pitford upended it for closer examination, it released an astonishing explosion of yellow excrement. Pitford was undeterred. He continued his study while Eugenia dabbed the mess from his sleeve with a scrap of embroidered handkerchief. Having made its feelings known, the bird lay supine in Pitford's hands as he parted feather and down, exclaiming upon the tail feathers ('Unusual, are they not? Bare barbed . . .'), the legs ('Clearly a bird accustomed to extensive foraging . . .'), oblivious to all else in his pleasure at this new acquisition.

Allbones had been standing by the wall, uncertain of his right to be there at all, partly concealed by a water butt, and it was there that Eugenia came to rinse the handkerchief clean.

'So,' she said, 'what do you think of our specimens, Mr Metcalfe?'

'Dunno, Miss,' said Allbones awkwardly. What was there to say? The birds were brown, they pecked and fluffed and were little different in his opinion to a couple of Mother Mossop's Orpingtons. 'They seem right enough, I suppose.'

'"Right enough"?' said Eugenia, and there was laughter in her voice, and ridicule. 'There are perhaps only another dozen like these in the whole country! My grandfather has gone to much trouble and expense to bring them here, from the other side of the world!'

'Is that so?' said Allbones. She thought him a poor fool. 'That'd be some way off then.'

'I should say so!' said Eugenia. A tendril of her hair had caught in the wind and brushed across his sleeve. 'I should say twelve thousand miles is a very great way off indeed!'

The second bird had joined its mate and the pair were striding off purposefully toward the painted mountains.

'One dozen hedgehogs!' said Pitford, rubbing his hands with satisfaction. 'Eh, Tweedie? One dozen unremarkable hedgehogs. Hotchkins such as one might find in any cottage garden, lending their modest aid to the cultivators of leeks and cabbages! And now they have found new employment in the gardens of the colony, while we have our woodhens. And, however useful the hedgehog may prove in his new home, I think we have the better bargain!'

The woodhens traced the limits of their domain, heads outstretched and tails flicking.

'They appear to be in good condition,' said Pitford.

'They have a good appetite, no doubt about that,' said Tweedie. 'They consumed a prodigious amount of potato on board — near on a hundredweight each, with scraps of salt pork, or fish, or rat or mouse or cockroach for garnish. They seem to be a most accommodating fowl!'

'So their maintenance should be straightforward,' said

Pitford. 'I shall give instructions to their keeper based on your recommendations. Perhaps we may discuss their care over dinner this evening?' He was moving away as he talked, escorting his guest toward the terrace. They passed Allbones as if he were indistinguishable from the water butt, and as they passed he saw Eugenia place her hand on the traveller's dusty sleeve and heard her say, 'A rogue wave! That must have been terrifying!', and the traveller's reply: 'Momentarily, as the ship turned on its side and threatened to submerge, perhaps, but the materials of scientific research are often gathered at great risk. The ornithologist Gilbert, for example, was massacred by Aboriginal savages while collecting in Australia . . .' The gate clicked shut.

Allbones was left standing with the two brown birds who were pecking with some curiosity at the strange leaves about their feet. In the neighbouring cage a black bird with a cluster of white feathers like a lacy knot at the neck was clinging to the netting.

It too was labelled: Allbones spelled the letters out laboriously: P R O S T H E M A D E R A N O V A E S E E L A N D I A E. No simple 'blackbird'. No uncomplicated 'thrush'. The bird with the long name regarded him from behind the netting with a jet-black bead of an eye.

'Hello,' it said.

As clearly as if it were human. Allbones looked over his shoulder. Surely it was Eugenia's voice? Perhaps she had returned unannounced and stood at his shoulder.

'Hello.'

The yard was empty, save for the birds in their cages.

'Hello.'

The girl's voice seemed to have flown over the wall,

separating itself from her person, and entered this bird. It opened its beak to expose a tongue like a tiny black brush.

'Hello,' it said. It tipped its head on one side as if anticipating a response.

Allbones moved closer. 'Hello,' he said.

The bird looked at him intently. 'Hello,' it replied.

'Oy!' called one of the stable-lads from the yard gate. 'I got to lock up!'

'Hello,' called the bird as Allbones hurried away down the alley between the cages. 'Hellohellohello!'

'Drive you mad, he will,' said the lad. 'Used to sing when he first came, but now it's just Hello hello and bleedin' hello.' He slammed the gate shut and slid the bolt home and Allbones headed for the trade gate while Eugenia's voice called after him — 'Hello! Hello!' — from behind the aviary wall.

3.

Dr Julius von Haast
Canterbury Museum
To William Docherty
Okarito
Oct. 13, 1870

	£	s	d
9 Ka Ka Pos	9	0	0
2 doz. Kiwi skins	7	4	0
1 doz. Kiwi skeletons	3	12	0
6 Rowi skins	6	0	0
4 Rowi skeletons	4	0	0
1 Ka Ka Po egg	10	0	
2 Kiwi eggs	1	0	0
2 Ka Ka Po skeletons	1	10	0
2 cases lined with tin	15	0	
26 Bird skins at 4/- each	7	4	0
	40	15	0

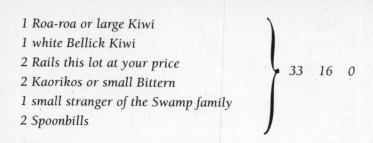

1 *Roa-roa or large Kiwi*
1 *white Bellick Kiwi*
2 *Rails this lot at your price*   } 33   16   0
2 *Kaorikos or small Bittern*
1 *small stranger of the Swamp family*
2 *Spoonbills*

Canterbury Museum Archives

The little cottage seethed with ferrets: polies and fitches with their black masks, sandies and whites, males and females, musky old hobs and playful kits scarcely out of the nest. They snapped and squealed or dozed, curled nose to paw among rags and straw. A butterbox below the window held two stoats, trapped near the swan's nest below the weir. They glowered sullen behind netting wire. Under the table three weasels scraped at the staves of a wooden bucket, squealing piteously for release. They had been the hardest to catch, being young and lively, but he'd got them at last with a vole skewered to some bent wire set in a ditch behind the church. He trapped at night after days at work clearing ditches. The rains had left tumbled banks and blockages in their wake and there had been no shortage of work, shovelling mud and muck. Pitford may have offered better money, but that was just for the summer, while the ditches came round regular, season after season, year after year. He bent to the shovel, heaving spoil aside, and kept a sharp ear out at snap time for any mention of breeders and baiters among the men who came for the ditching from away.

By the end of the fortnight the cottage smelled richly of musk and the squealing and fighting kept the littl'uns awake at nights.

'You're not to breathe a word of this,' he said to them as they stood on tiptoe to investigate the contents of the barrel or dangled a bootlace through the wire to tease the stoats. 'This is no one's business but our own. No blash, no blather, eh?' And he tapped them each smartly with the wooden spoon so they would remember. They yelped but the tears dried quickly to snail trails on grubby cheeks, ignored in the fascination at all this activity released so unexpectedly in their very own kitchen.

Allbones surveyed his stock with satisfaction. Two shillings a head he'd paid for the sandies from a breeder over Netherton way, a burly bankin-man with his big banking boots hung by the step and a skinny lurcher stretched in a patch of sunlight by the ash-house. Allbones had walked out there on Sunday afternoon and found him at work in his garden. The bankin-man was not a frequenter of the King's Arms and did not recognise him. He was suspicious, digging away at his potato shaws with a steady resolution not to be drawn.

'Don't know what you're talking about, man,' he said, turning a spadeful of heavy earth. 'You've got the wrong name. Ferrets? Not me.' The lurcher stretched luxuriously, moaning with pleasure at the dream chase, its paws racing over dream grass after dream rabbits. Its yellow teeth chattered. The yard smelled of turned earth and sweat and ale on the breath and potatoes laid out ready for planting, but underlying all was the unmistakable odour of ferret. Many ferrets.

Allbones leaned against the wall and undid his necker-chief. From a knotted corner he removed a sovereign. It glinted in the sun and the bankin-man's back straightened. He laid aside his spade.

'But if it's just a couple you need, like, to deal to the rats . . .' He led the way between ranks of seedling cabbages and peas on crossed stakes to a shed behind some currant bushes. The kind of shed where tools might be kept and sharpened. He opened the door and the stink poured forth from rows of cages, each housing a sleepy occupant blinking in the sudden light from its nest of straw.

The bankin-man took Allbones for a novice, one who might be fobbed off with some sluts in a cage of their own at the back of the shed where the shadows were deepest. Young females, he said, fresh and ready for rabbiting. Allbones checked them over briefly: torn ears, scratched muzzles, they flinched at the least touch, bearing the bruises of a busy season. Skulkers and killers probably, who ate rather than bolting the rabbit. Or intractable, not readily handled, not settling quiet in the pocket.

'No,' he said, and he made his own selection. 'That one, and that one, and these . . .' choosing from the cages nearest the door, where anyone would keep their best stock, handy to scoop up on a dark night. The bankin-man was hesitant, but the coin glinted and he had a powerful thirst and finally they reached an agreement. Ten sandies and no awkward questions. He took the sovereign and called out to his wife that he was just off to show the visitor on his way and he'd be back like smack. A distant 'Ha!' from an upstairs window was all her reply — she'd heard that before — and they set off together, just as far as the end cottage, which, to judge from the chat and clink within, doubled as a public house. There the bankin-man said it had been a pleasure doing business with him and best of luck, before tapping three times at the closed door. He was inside before Allbones had turned the corner.

The sun had set long before he reached home and the road shone white under a full moon veiled in little hen scrattins of cloud. He walked the four miles with heavy pockets between hawthorn hedges just breaking into the creamy lick of blossom. That night the sandies took up temporary residence in a barrel he had prepared for them with straw and mice and some nestling thrushes.

Another nine, the fitches, came from the opposite direction, a rundown farmlet in the middle of a turnip field, a white crown still showing here and there like a bare skull in the mud and dead leaves flapping surrender. A woman did the haggling here. A sharp little woman with hair scraped so tight her scaly pink scalp showed between the strands. Her husband stood by while she argued for sixpence a head more. His eyes were milky with glaucoma: a labourer, who'd enjoyed his rabbiting before his vision clouded, she said. Took good care of his ferrets, didn' you, George? Coped them all hisself, didn' you, George? Filin' them eye teeth down so's they couldn' bite, doin' it all by touch when he couldn' see what his fingers was up to. Gentled them all from the nest. But they was going to have to leave now the rents was goin' up an' move in with their son and his wife and his wife couldn' abide ferrets, said she'd as soon have rats about the place as a mess of ferrets, and it was a shame, but there you were . . .

The cages were deep in dirty straw and the wood was rotting from the accumulation of acid dung, but the animals seemed healthy nevertheless. Allbones checked them over carefully; their eyes were bright, the pads on their paws were soft and pink. No signs of mange, but the minute he got them home he'd dunk them in the pot of lard and sulphur he kept beneath the bench, just to be sure. The woman chattered on while her husband listened, arguing the case for two and sixpence a head, they was that strong, never a touch of pneumonie or the sniffles, kept nice and warm and raised on the fat of the land . . .

Allbones gave her her sixpence. They were good stock, after all. She grabbed the coins as if they might evaporate before she got her fingers around them, all smiles. Then she fussed over each ferret before dropping it into his pocket, calling it 'darlin'' and instructing it to be good on its way to its new home. She exclaimed over the distance he had come that day (he had lied and told her Netherton in the interests of discretion), she offered him a cup of tea before he left and when he said no, released a volley of 'Are you certain's and 'It'd be no trouble's, but finally she was standing on the step arm in arm with George to wave goodbye and Allbones could escape with his cargo.

By Friday he had them all: thirty ferrets. Nineteen sluts and eleven hobs, all in good health, all vigorous and suitable for emigration. He stowed them in his pockets or in little drawstring bags Mary Anne had sewn to keep them each separate in the sack. The stoats and weasels he carried in two small boxes tightly fastened. Laden with his stock, he let himself out quietly while it was yet dark and no one in the Bottom End was up and doing. No clatter of pattens came from the lane, nor the rumble of wagon wheels and the steady tread of feathered horse hooves as the labourers set off for the fields. No flutter of curtain edge at Mother Mossop's watchful window. The moon shone feebly in decline with the morning stars gathered all about, and the air had that breathless quality that had yet to be broken by some rooster standing tiptoe on a dungheap, laying down its challenge to the day. Allbones kept to the shadows with his boxes and bundle, hugging the hedgerows. Everything was soaked with dew as if the river had risen overnight and swamped the whole valley: woods and fields had surely been submerged and eels had woven their way between elm and oak. Houses had sunk until only the chimneypots were visible, and the people sleeping within had drifted, hair afloat on the rafts that had been their beds, dreaming soft undulating dreams. Flower and leaf and hawthorn blossom hung on their stems like sodden scraps and, before he had been walking five minutes, his trousers too were soaked, hanging heavy-cuffed as if he had been wading up to the knees.

He encountered no one on the road. Undetected, he reached the proper gate just as the sky began to lighten along its eastern edge and the day birds stirred. He had hours to wait, so he climbed a stile into a field. Cowslips grew there in profusion, smelling sweet and damp, but under the hedge he found a pile of worked stones that had once been someone's home where he could sit and wait as the world turned from grey and white to green and blue and yellow and a pair of cuckoos set up their regular *ticktock*. He took out his piece of bread and rind and ate his breakfast. The sack lay across his lap, and he could feel the warmth of all those small bodies, lulled by the rhythm of his walking to sleep. Beyond the hedge a wagon lumbered by, the driver whistling tunelessly. *Ticktock* went the cuckoos. *Ticktock ticktock*. By and by, the sun reached over the hedge and found its way down to where Allbones leaned against a mossy stone. His eyes grew heavy.

When he woke it was, by his nearest guess, mid-morning. Insects hummed in the hawthorn and some light gig drawn by a smart horse with a high-stepping tread was passing by on the road. It clipped off briskly around the corner in the direction of Brinkton. Allbones gathered up the sack and straightened his coat, brushed dead leaves from his trousers and, for the first time, passed openly through the iron gates into the grounds of the big house. He walked with a fine legitimacy to the stable-yard, where a man was grooming a big bay cob, hissing as he brushed its coat to a fine gleam.

'Mr Donnithorne?' the man said without missing a stroke. 'Over there.' He jutted his chin in the direction of a low building against the aviary wall. 'Hello! Hello!' cried the bird from behind the barricade. The yard smelled rich and clean, of horse and straw and the fine resinous scent of freshly sawn timber.

Mr Donnithorne stood at a bench tacking netting to a cage. A couple of lads were sawing a length of elm. A cliff face of crates was stacked against one wall, each neatly netted and carpeted with dry shavings. Donnithorne was another who did not welcome interruption. He looked up briefly and continued working, lips clenched about a row of staples like silver fangs. He was a miserable long wisp of a man, stooped and balding, with shavings caught in strands of fair hair scraped over the crown. His nose was long and pendulous and from its tip a drip hung like an icicle from a cornice.

At last he was done. He stood back, eyed his handiwork mournfully, then added the crate to the pile.

'Metcalfe, is it?' he said. 'Thought somethin' must have happened to you. An accident, like. Drownded. Kicked by a 'oss.' His voice wheezed, his rheumy eyes watered copiously. He seemed to be permanently in tears, to doubt that the world could ever be set true. He took a rag from his trouser pocket and blew hugely and wetly, then peered at the effluvia. 'These cages is a right fiddlefaddle,' he said. 'Prob'ly won' do either. Bound to be somethin' lackin.'

'They look big enough,' said Allbones, who had never seen such perfect accommodation for ferrets in his life. His own stock, certainly, had never known such luxury. 'Good an' roomy.'

'Two foot wide, by a foot high and one and a half deep,' said Donnithorne. 'Should be space for three or four easy.'

'They don' allus settle,' said Allbones. 'Mebbe only one to the cage, or two if you're lucky. Hobs is allus kept single, else they'll fight.' He examined one of the cages more closely. 'How do you get 'em in?' he said. 'Or feed an' water?'

'Openin's 'inged,' said Donnithorne, demonstrating. The netting side gaped wide.

'Won't do,' said Allbones. 'You'll never keep 'em. Top trap's the only way, small as you can manage and still get your hand in. An' weasels'll need narrower-gauge wire. They'll be through that before you can blink.'

A drop from Donnithorne's nose fell among the shavings on the floor.

'Din' think they'd do,' he said. 'Din' I say before we started, lads?'

Yes, said the lads, he had said so.

Allbones set the sack down on the floor and drew a poley from one of his pockets. It wriggled furiously, black eyes blinking in the sudden light. Donnithorne held one cage open.

'Nothin's ever straightforrard,' he said. 'There's allus a catch.' The poley leapt into its new quarters and burrowed into the shavings, squeaking with alarm.

'They don' like bein' watched,' said Allbones. 'They're secretive, like. You'll need more shavin's or straw where they can hide, lots of it, and they'll need dungin' out regular or their piss'll rot the wood.'

'Prob'ly won' last the distance,' mourned Donnithorne. 'Months them ferrets got to live in them cages. Months out on the sea. Prob'ly get washed overboard before they gets there. Hear that, lads? Their piss rots the wood. Cages'll be fallen to pieces in no time and all our work for nothing.'

Allbones drew one of the sandies from another pocket and Donnithorne held open another inadequate cage. But the sandie was restless, unnerved by the polie's squealing. The instant it was released it made a bid for freedom, straight up the netting before Donnithorne could close the catch. It scrambled out over the top and fell to the ground, where it found the safe dark tunnel that was the left cuff of Donnithorne's trousers. Up it went, scaling the trunk of his skinny leg as he grabbed at knee, thigh, then groin where the ferret, terrified, sank its needle teeth into the soft scrotal sac.

'Aaah!' screamed Donnithorne, long legs capering about the yard, body doubled over, hands fumbling frantically at fly buttons. 'Yer bastard!' The two lads left their sawing and rushed to the doorway to watch.

'That's some jig you're doin' there, Mr Donnithorne!' called one, while the other laughed. 'Bow to the left and bow to the right. One two three! One two three . . .'

'In the trough!' shouted Allbones over the racket. 'Sit in the trough! It'll not let go till it's under water!' Through all the noise he was aware of a gate opening in the high stone wall behind them and the sound of laughter, lighter than the lads' loud guffaws. A rippling amusement at the sight of the old man prancing, cursing, leaping in the general direction of the stableyard trough. A girl's laughter.

With a final despairing cry Donnithorne half stumbled, half jumped into the scummy water, where he sank back like a man taking his bath. Once submerged, the sandie had no option but to release its grip. It rose to the surface, paddling madly for the concrete edging as if walking on water, and was over and off under the stable end.

Donnithorne lay back, eyes closed, hands delicately cradling his wounded parts, emitting loud groans. 'They carries disease,' he mourned. 'Bite like that, I stands to lose my manhood!'

'Like I was sayin',' said Allbones, kneeling to peer under the stable where the ferret had vanished into darkness, 'top openin's the only way.' Four shillings gone and there would be no catching it now. Once frightened they became wary. On his knees, ridiculous, he could hear the ripple of laughter at his back.

Donnithorne scrambled to his feet in sodden trousers. 'Don' know what's so funny about flesh rottin' and a man dyin',' he said, the rebuke directed at the lads, who stood smirking at the workshop door, and at her, too, this young miss who had emerged from the aviary to laugh, in her blue smock spattered with paint. 'Don' know that there's anythin' amusin' in a man losin' his livelihood, his family to the poor house, his bairns fatherless. Don' think that's amusin' at all.' He dripped and mourned.

'You'll not die from a bite,' said Allbones, peering into the dark to see if he could make out a pair of red eyes glaring back suspiciously from a far corner.

'It can happen,' said Donnithorne. 'I heard of a man bit by a squirrel on a Sunday. Dead by Tuesday. I'll ask at the house for Mercurochrome, but I don' hold much hope. An' you . . .' he directed a foul look at the lads in the doorway, '. . . get back to your work instead of standin' round gawpin'.'

The rhythmic grinding of saw teeth on timber fell into the space that opened between the girl standing by the gate and Allbones kneeling at the stable wall and Donnithorne walking tenderly and already rehearsing his own funeral toward the kitchen door.

Allbones heard the tap of small boots on the cobblestones behind him.

'So that was the action of a ferret!' she said. 'They move with great speed, do they not?'

'They do,' said Allbones, giving up on retrieval and standing up. 'Specially when they're feared.'

'Can I help you put them in their cages?' said Eugenia.

'Best not, Miss,' said Allbones. 'It's mucky work.'

She held up her hands, all smeared with paint.

'I'm already mucky,' she said, mimicking Allbones' pronunciation. 'I'll open the cages and you can drop them in. How many do you have?'

'Eight in my pockets,' said Allbones. 'Twenty in the sack.'

Eugenia undid a latch. 'Thirty in just twelve days!' she said. 'My grandfather will be delighted!' She held the cage door ajar, while Allbones took a ferret from his coat pocket and transferred it to its new quarters.

'Twenty-nine now,' said Allbones, 'and scant chance of catching the thirtieth again. It'll stay put and not come back to risk being half-drownded again.'

'So they are intelligent creatures?' said Eugenia. Another ferret, a poley, was slipped into its home and the door swiftly latched behind it.

'Yes,' said Allbones. 'They're hunters. They outwit.'

He opened the box containing the stoats and managed to pick one up by the scruff so that it swung in his fist, hissing and wriggling. It was necessary to pay close attention if they were to judge exactly the moment to release the animal, withdraw the hand, slam the netting shut. It required them to stand close, and it was perhaps inevitable that Allbones' hand should brush Eugenia's and that Eugenia's fingers should touch his. He could smell fresh linen, soap, oil paint and violets. And once more that stillness fell: no sawing from the rear of the workshop, no stamping of horses' hooves from the stable across the yard, just a tiny instant when everything held its breath.

The stoat nipped as it leapt for the straw, enough to leave a single bubble of blood on Allbones' thumb and to break the silence.

'You been makin' pictures?' he said.

'Pictures?' said Eugenia.

'Paintin' an' that,' said Allbones. The second stoat joined the first in its cage without fuss.

'Yes. Indeed I have. I've been painting. Makin' pictures,' she said and he could hear again that laughter in the mimicry. 'A forest backdrop on one of the aviary cages. It is very difficult. All the botanical detail must be absolutely correct.'

Allbones turned his attention to the sack. The knot was tied fast: it had become wet that morning and could not be budged. He fumbled and tugged and said nothing in reply. He'd give this girl no more grounds for ridicule.

'And most of the specimens I have to work from are dried and pressed. So it is not easy to imagine their original colour and setting.' She paused. She seemed to expect some response

83

but Allbones kept busy, picking apart damp fibre with clumsy, calloused fingers. 'I do it well,' she said. 'My grandfather says that in time I may rival Mrs Gould.'

The words shone with self-importance. And meant nothing to Allbones whatsoever.

'I may be permitted to illustrate one of his books,' she said when he remained silent. 'He writes on the subject of rarity and extinction, particularly among the island species of the South Pacific.'

Allbones picked and tugged.

'He is one of the foremost authorities,' she said.

Allbones gave up. He took his knife from his pocket, the knife with three blades that he had lifted from a shelf in Ledney when he was still a lad and running messages for a penny for anyone needing a note delivered. The knife had lain unattended while its owner fumbled in a dresser drawer for his spectacles, too preoccupied to notice as this urchin pocketed his trophy and made off for the cover of the woods. He buried it under an oak tree and resisted the impulse to dig it up for several months, until the searching was all over. The man was gentle and reluctant to accuse, to question the veracity of the poor. He was forgetful besides, and doubted his own memory. Maybe he had dropped it himself on his morning walk? Left it on a stile or the top of a wall, so stupid, so careless . . .

By the time Allbones dug it up it had rusted a little, but the blades still flipped sharp from the sheath. Three blades — one large, one small, one serrated — a corkscrew, a hoof pick, an awl, and a couple of blades he did not know the exact purpose for, which nevertheless came in handy for picking at things: locks, for instance. The horn handle, adorned with a silver shield, held a tiny pair of tweezers. Also useful.

The knife was his greatest treasure. He kept it clean, wiping off all traces of mud or blood, and stored it, wrapped in a scrap of woollen cloth, behind a brick in the wall of the ash house, where it might be retrieved readily before any expedition. And out of reach so that none of the littl'uns could come upon it and take it for play and lose it.

He opened the largest blade, feeling the customary pleasure in its smooth steel strength as it sliced through the tangle as readily as it slid through muscle and flesh.

The sack gaped open.

'But then,' said the girl, 'you've probably never heard of Mrs Gould.'

'No,' said Allbones, taking a masked hob from its draw-string bag. It squirmed, hind legs fighting for purchase, then in its fright released a fine spray of musk over the girl's smock. The stink drenched the air, but she seemed unperturbed. She did not squeal as some might have done, or run to sponge the marks away, but continued to hold the cage door ajar as if nothing untoward had happened.

'And the Pacific?' she enquired. 'You do know of the Pacific?'

'Don' know, don' need to know,' said Allbones. Did she take him for a complete fool?

'It is a vast ocean, occupying a full third of the globe, stretching from Asia to America,' said Eugenia.

'Izzat a fact?' said Allbones. He had another ferret by the neck.

'Yes,' said Eugenia. 'It contains many islands, and on these islands vast numbers of species have evolved in curious ways . . .' She paused. 'But perhaps you don't know about evolution either,' she said. 'Perhaps you've never heard of Darwin?'

'Can' say as I have,' said Allbones. Of course he had heard of Mr Darwin. A faint recollection of the devil invoked by the vicar in long, vehement sermons back when Allbones was dragged to church by his ma, to sit drumming his heels in the stall by the door where the field women sat, cracked hands folded meekly in torn mittens. The crude cartoon of a man with a top hat and a tail like an organ grinder's monkey. He had heard of Darwin all right, but he felt disinclined to say so. If she chose to think him a fool, very well, he'd play the fool.

'Oh dear,' she said, as if he were a three-year-old and she a woman of vast maturity and learning. 'Where can one start?'

'You can open them cages,' said Allbones, with a couple of skinny sandies in his grasp.

Eugenia seemed serenely unoffended. She undid the latch. 'So I take it you believe the world and all its creatures were moulded by the Creator in just seven days?'

'Can' say I've given it much thought,' said Allbones. She was so self-important, this girl, so full of herself.

'But you must have wondered about the animals and plants about you in the woods, and how they have taken their present forms?' she said. 'You must have some beliefs?'

Allbones shrugged. 'Things are what they are,' he said. 'I don' trouble my head further.'

'Well,' said Eugenia, placing her hands fingertip to fingertip in a gesture Allbones recognised immediately as being in imitation of her grandfather when he was about to impart some morsel of information. 'Things are not simply just "what they are". At least they do not remain so. Everything alive is changing in little ways that we, who are changing ourselves, cannot detect . . .'

He let her talk, steadily moving along the row of cages,

keeping his attention on the task in hand, housing ferret after ferret. She assisted, talking all the while.

'All living forms are engaged in a struggle for existence. Should any individual possess features that give it some advantage in that struggle, it will have a better chance of survival; it will be fittest to pass those characteristics to its offspring. And after . . . oh . . .' she waved her hand airily, 'ages and ages . . . there will evolve by the processes of natural selection, that immense variation we observe about us. Birds with beaks perfectly adapted to capture insects and birds with beaks to catch fish and . . . so on.'

The sack was empty. The ferrets were burrowed already into the wood shavings or examining their new homes with their customary insatiable curiosity, pink noses wrinkling, pink eyes scanning for any way out.

'And that,' said Eugenia, wiping her hands on her pinafore, 'is Darwin's theory of evolution by natural selection.' She was pleased with her lecture.

'They'll need to be fed mornin' and evenin',' said Allbones, folding up the sack. 'Fresh meat only. They won' touch what's dead an' dry. Mice'll do 'em, or rabbit, anythin' so long as it's still runnin' with blood.'

He could sense the covert scrutiny of the lads at the sawbench. He could hear muttered asides and muffled sniggering. Donnithorne had not reappeared and he had not received his promised advance, but he wanted desperately to be done and away from here, where he felt trapped between talkative condescension on the one hand and satirical observation on the other.

'I'd best be goin',' he said. 'Thanks for your help. You'll be wantin' to get back to your pictures.'

Eugenia looked suddenly shy. Just a girl, really, and not half as grown up in her ways as Mary Anne, who had been out on her own in the world.

'Would you like to see them?' she said. And blushed furiously. 'My pictures?' This time she did not mimic. 'I'd like to show them to you, if you're interested. In return for showing us the cubs.'

Allbones had the sack bundled, his pockets were emptied, ferret, stoat and weasel were all safely stowed in their cages, he could leave if he chose. But the girl seemed so eager. Where a moment ago he had felt only irritation with her, now he felt something like a stirring of sympathy.

'I've never shown them to anyone before,' she said. 'Apart from my grandfather, of course.'

Allbones still hesitated. Eugenia saw him pause and made her own judgement concerning his reasons for caution. 'My grandfather won't mind. He has gone to Brinkton. He won't return till the afternoon.'

Her eyes were blue and very earnest. She stood in her stained pinafore, hands clasped. Just a young girl, pleased with her work and wanting to show it to someone, the way he felt when he'd finished making a net and it all fell true and folded neatly for the pocket. Or when a night had gone well and his pockets hung heavy and he walked homeward, thinking of the moment where he drew the rabbits from his coat like a magician and Mary Anne clapped her hands and danced about the room. Everyone wants to share their handiwork when they've done their best.

'All right,' he said.

Eugenia smiled, all delight, recovering her former assurance. 'They're very good!' she said as she led the way through the aviary gates, the mocking whistles of the lads — by-wipes the pair of them — a muffled accompaniment.

The aviary was filled with fluttering and squawking. The two brown birds were pecking at a trough of barley like a pair of barnyard fowl, and the black bird swooped to meet them.

'Hello!' it shrilled, hopping along a dry branch. 'Hello!' It echoed Eugenia exactly.

The cage next to it was empty, but on its rear wall had been sketched the outlines of a waterfall tumbling among ferns, and the sky was already a wash of brilliant blue.

'Blue is my favourite colour,' said Eugenia. 'I prefer it to all others. What is your favourite colour?'

'Dunno,' said Allbones. Her hair was pale like wheat when it was near ripe and shimmering as the wind passed over it. Her skin was white as a china cup, one of those delicate breakable things women seemed to love, the kind of thing his mother would sigh over at the market, holding one tenderly to examine it more closely and ignoring the stall owner's glare and his curt, 'You break that, Missus, you pays for it.' She would hold up the cup and say, 'Look at that, Walter! Bone china! You can see the light right through!' The cup was made of bones, dead things, all dried and crushed and turned to something that let the light through. That was the colour of Eugenia's skin. And her lips were the colour of the roses that were painted in profusion on such china cups.

'You must have a favourite,' she insisted. 'My grandfather favours crimson.'

Allbones shrugged. 'Never thought about it,' he said, but thinking as he said it of the blue of a kingfisher's wing as it dives, the silver of the fish wriggling in its beak, the pale green of new willow, the corduroy brown of a field ploughed and rimed with frost.

'The sky above the Pacific is reputed to be the most brilliant of all blues,' said Eugenia. 'Cerulean blue, azure and turquoise. I hope I have rendered it accurately.'

She stood close by, only half a pace before him, judging her work. Her neck was bare for she had tied up her hair roughly with a purple scarf. He could reach out, run one finger lightly down the tiny bumps of the spine, trace the hollows on either side and touch the tips of her ears. He forced his hands down into his pockets and sought to distract them with chat.

'It looks good,' he said. 'Real, like.'

'Thank you,' she said. Her pale skin flushed with pleasure.

'How do you know what to paint?' said Allbones, hands tightly clenched.

'My grandfather describes the setting to me from some traveller's account, then I close my eyes and the pictures simply float into my head,' she said, closing her eyes as she spoke. Her lashes fluttered on her cheeks. 'Some of these backdrops are not as well executed as they should be. I was younger when I painted them, and inexperienced. The book illustrations are much more difficult, for they will be examined closely by naturalists and scientists. They must be absolutely correct. Come: I'll show you.'

She led the way along the terrace and opened one of the tall doors into the long room. Still the clock ticking, the fire burning in the grate, the scents of polished wood and leather bindings and tobacco and paint. On the corner table, the tall brown bird among the bulrushes had been displaced by two black birds on an arrangement of twigs and dry leaf. They resembled rooks or crows, except that these rooks had creamy wattles and a broad strip of white to their tail feathers. One faced the wall and had a beak that was short and blunt, while the other faced the window and had a beak that was curving and slender, like the sickles the bankin-men used for cutting reeds. Their outline had already been partially translated to a sheet of heavy paper pinned to the dais.

'These are my new models,' said Eugenia, stroking the birds' glossy heads. '*Heteralocha acutirostris*. This is the female — an oddity in nature because she possesses the more remarkable beak, when generally it is the male who is dramatic, while the female, being coy, remains discreet and barely distinguishable from the young of her species. But they're perfectly matched, because the male employs his blunt beak to break open the rotten wood containing the slugs on which they feed, while the female is naturally equipped to draw them forth. Curious, are they not?'

'Yes,' said Allbones. Curious and beautiful. The birds, with their glossy green-black feathers. The girl in her blue smock. The room with its many curiosities.

'These are the birds my grandfather hopes to receive in exchange for your ferrets,' she said. 'No one has yet managed to transport a living pair, but he plans to bring them here, to breed in our aviary. But in the meantime, I must work from these models.'

Eugenia held up a thick black crayon. 'I sketch first, and if my drawing is good enough I am allowed to copy it to a stone . . .' She pointed to a slab of finely grained limestone that lay beside the dais, '. . . using this crayon. Then my grandfather sends my drawing to a printer in London whom he considers the best in his trade. And he inks the stone and produces two hundred or more copies which I colour, using these specimens for reference. And that is how the illustrations for a book are made.'

She was pleased with her drawing, with her understanding.

'Drawing is my one great talent,' she went on. 'I am tone
deaf, just as I have no sense of smell. Can't smell a thing, can't
tell one note from another, can't sing or play the piano.
Fortunately my grandfather considers those frivolous occupa-
tions. He tutors me himself in mathematics and science and I
am competent enough, though I have difficulty with prose,
whereas he is a great stylist. But I can draw. I am hoping that
this illustration, for example, might be good enough to be
included in his book. His great catalogue. His definitive study
of extinction.'

'What's that then?' said Allbones.

'Extinction,' she said. 'All these creatures are doomed.'
She gestured toward the perfectly matched crows. 'These . . .
and those and those.' Waving at the cabinets with their little
frozen imitations of life.

She pulled open one of the shallow drawers.

'And these . . .' The drawer was full of small birds: tiny
finches of purest yellow or speckled brown and buff, robins of
deepest black or flashed with white, birds that resembled
tomtits and dunnocks, but larger or smaller or spotted and
striped in novel fashion.

'And these . . .' said Eugenia. Another drawer containing
owls, their round eye sockets empty. Drawer after drawer of
empty skins, each skin with the wings tightly furled and its
claws laid reverently along the gash in the breast, like a child
whose hands have been arranged in prayer made ready for
Christian burial. Each with a cardboard tag tied to one claw.
Falcons and harriers with blunt heads and savage beaks, dusky

green parrots, some as big as cats, some tiny with caps of brilliant gold or scarlet or blue, penguins with white breast feathers and big red paddling feet, a snowy egret over two foot tall, ducks and scaup and herons the colour of water on a cloudy day, seabirds white as foam and waders with spindly red legs. Other drawers held their eggs, in nests of cottonwool: rows of blue and brown and cream, some speckled, some the size of a thimble and some larger than any egg Allbones had ever seen, larger than the eggs of swan or goose. Some were cut in two to reveal the thick wall of the shell, and all had that tiny perfect hole from which yolk and albumen had been sucked clean.

'All doomed,' she said. She liked the drama of it. 'Soon there will be no evidence of their existence other than collections such as this one and the records of science.'

'Why?' said Allbones. 'What's doomin' them?'

Eugenia shrugged. 'Nature,' she said. 'Just as England's shorthorn cattle take the place of other breeds wherever they have been introduced because of their superior vigour in the production of meat and milk, so these birds are encountering the blackbirds and starlings of the English countryside, transported for the pleasure of their song or their utility by emigrants. It is a law of nature that competition for resources is fiercest between those creatures that most resemble one another, and in this battle the indigenous species are destined to fail.'

She closed a drawer on its cargo of ducks — little blue-black ducks, brown ducks and grey ducks — shovel beaks tucked close, paddles pressed flat as a dead leaf. The drawer emitted a puff of that duck scent of oily feather and pond-weed and limpid lakes on icy mornings, overlaid with the camphorated smell of arsenical preservative.

'My grandfather says we are enormously fortunate to be living in this era. Extinction normally takes ages and ages, but in the islands of the Pacific, so recently settled, science has the perfect laboratory to examine the process at close quarters. Just think, Mr Metcalfe! Soon there will be nothing left of these creatures but bones in a museum. To know anything of their habits, scientists in another hundred years will have to consult my grandfather's books. And to understand their appearance in life, they will examine my illustrations! My "pictures"!'

Her face was pink with enthusiasm, her eyes shining.

'So, all these birds is dyin'?' said Allbones.

'Some are already extinct,' said Eugenia. 'Others are fast becoming so.'

The two black crows sat on the corner table clamped to their branch in a parody of courtship, their bright eyes made of glass, their breasts plumped around wire and woollen stuffing.

'What a pity,' said Allbones.

'Pity has nothing to do with it,' said Eugenia. She opened another drawer: a skinned flock of peculiar long-beaked birds he did not recognise, clad in shaggy brown coats. 'It's not a matter for emotion. In the struggle of existence some species press hard on varieties less adapted for survival. It's pointless to care one way or the other. It is useful only to observe and record as accurately as one can.'

'But they're beautiful,' said Allbones, and flushed the minute the words had left his mouth for they sounded soft.

'Maybe,' she said, 'but that's also irrelevant. It's as pointless to regret the death of something we consider beautiful as to lament the death of a slug.'

'Don't be daft,' said Allbones. 'If a bird dies, singing its heart out and flying up and up into the sky, you'd feel the loss of it in a way you'd never feel sad at stepping on some ugly great slug.'

'You can feel that way,' said Eugenia, 'but nature won't care one way or the other. Nature is concerned only with survival. The bird with the strongest beak or the longest legs or the best-defended nest survives, and that is all that matters. Not beauty. What's beauty anyway? How do you define it?'

'I can see it,' said Allbones.

'Oh yes?' said Eugenia. She is standing before the window and the light is making her hair a glistening halo, like a dandelion head when you hold it up to blow away the hours.

'For instance, you're beautiful,' he said.

Eugenia looked around at him. 'Am I?' she said, as if it had never occurred to her before, as if no one had ever told her.

'Yes,' said Allbones, her surprise making him bold. 'You are. Your face is beautiful. Your hair is beautiful. You have beautiful lips and beautiful eyes.'

She had opened a drawer full of cormorants: black and white and grey-spotted and one pure white, each one toppled from a tree on a distant coast and swiftly collected, sliced from breastbone to vent, each joint severed, the skin drawn up and over the head as easily as taking off a shirt, the brain scooped out with a tarnished spoon, the skin rubbed with preservative then folded to a tidy rectangle, fit for packing in a box with dozens of its dry dead kind . . . She stood very still as his right hand emerged from his pocket and seemingly without his control made its own way to touch her neck: the hollows beneath the hairline, the tiny bumps of the spine . . .

But before he could quite reach her there was some bustle

in the hall, the sound of voices, the rapid stamp of boots crossing a parquet floor. Eugenia shut the drawer swiftly and Allbones turned as the door was flung open and Pitford strode into the room. He paused on seeing them, in the midst of removing his gloves.

'Mr Metcalfe has brought the ferrets,' said Eugenia, moving quickly to take his hat and cane. 'He has been waiting to talk to you about their care and feeding.'

'Donnithorne will attend to that,' said Pitford curtly. 'And Metcalfe here could have waited outside.'

'I wanted to show him my drawing of the huia,' said Eugenia. 'In return for showing us the badgers.'

Pitford laid his gloves on the desk.

'You wanted to show him this?' he said. He walked deliberately to the desk and removed the drawing, taking each pin from its corner. He held it up and considered it critically, then slowly, as if drawing the pelt from a dead animal, he tore it in two. Eugenia stood by watching, all the colour draining from her face as he dropped the pieces into the wastepaper basket.

'I don't think your work is quite ready yet for public display,' he said. Eugenia made no sound. She stooped and gathered up the ruined pieces from the basket, then left the room, not glancing in Allbones' direction. The door clicked shut and there was the sound of her feet running up the stairs.

Pitford opened the doors to the terrace.

'So,' he said, 'you have brought the first consignment. And since you have waited, perhaps we should take a look at them.'

The ferrets peered from their cages, pink noses whiffling.

Pitford made a rapid tally. 'Only twenty-nine,' he said.

'I lost one on the way,' said Allbones. Donnithorne stood

morosely hammering a nail home, bent a little gingerly from the waist.

'The amount will be deducted from your next advance,' said Pitford.

'He says the cages isn't right, Mr Pitford,' said Donnithorne. 'Top-openin' it's got to be, and one cage each, else they'll fight. That's a lot more cages than was reckoned for.'

'If Metcalfe here says it is necessary, then it probably is,' said Pitford. 'He is the expert on these matters.'

Donnithorne looked sourly at Allbones.

'I'm sure he is, sir,' he said.

'And a deeper litter,' said Allbones. 'They like to be snug, like us humans do. And if the females come on heat, they'll need matin' or they'll die. And you'll need to keep a watch on the hobs when they're put to the slut — and you must always do it that way, never the slut to the hob or he could kill her — and you'll need to watch 'em because some hobs don't know when to stop and they'll need draggin' off before the slut is ruined. They're healthy stock, I've checked them all, but if any of them takes sick — off their food, like, an' the pads on their feet feel hard to the touch — then that's the distemper and you'll need to cull 'em without a moment's delay or you'll lose the lot.'

'Got all that, Donnithorne?' said Pitford.

'Yes, sir,' said Donnithorne, wiping his nose on a rag and looking more miserable then ever. 'They're goin' to need a lot of carin'.'

'So, twenty a week,' said Pitford, 'from now till the end of September. Four shilling a head, paid on delivery. And should the stock prove inferior in any way, our agreement is cancelled forthwith. I shall check them myself. Is that clear?'

'Yes, sir,' said Allbones as Pitford turned on his heel and, good humour restored, strode back toward the house.

Allbones took his four pounds in small coins counted cautiously by the reluctant Donnithorne and let himself out of the yard. As he fixed the latch he looked up at the house and thought he saw a lonely figure at a window on the second floor.

'Hello!' cried the bird in the voice that was foreign to it and not its own native tongue.

He might have been mistaken in seeing her there. It may have been just the fluttering of a curtain or the reflection of a cloud, passing over the glass.

4.

Collector, Location & Collecting Period	No. of birds (skins and mounts)	Specialities	Current Location
W. Rothschild, Tring, England, 1880–1931	280,000	World	AMNH
A.O. Hume, Simla, India, 1862–1885	102,000	Indian Empire	BMNH
W.H. Phelps, Caracas, Venezuela, 1897–1965	70,000	S. America Esp. Venezuela	Phelps Museum Caracas
J. Dwight, New York City, 1897–1930	65,000	N. and C. America	AMNH

H. von Berlepsch, Cassel, Germany, 1868–1915	55,000	S. America, Palearctic hummingbirds	Senckenberg Museum Frankfurt am Main
A. Boucard, Paris and London, 1839–1904	43,000	World, esp. C. America	MNHN Paris
G. M. Mathews, Watford, England, 1902–1918	30,000	Australia	AMNH
H. B. Tristram, Durham, England, 1840s–1906	24,000	World, esp. Mid. East Pacific Is.	Liverpool

Et cetera . . .

From a table recording 'The Great Accumulators' in Barbara and Richard Mearns, The Bird Collectors, Academic Press, 1998.

AMNH – American Museum of Natural History
BMNH – British Museum of Natural History
MNHN – Museum National d'Histoire Naturelle

'What you been up to?' said Fowler, his bulk jamming the narrow doorway. Allbones knelt back on his heels in his shadow. (He had been hammering toeplates onto the soles of his new boots: boots from the bootmaker in Brinkton, so that he could now go out shod like some gentleman's prize hunter with freshly oiled hooves.)

'This 'n that,' he said.

The boots gleamed in contradiction. When had Allbones ever been seen in new boots and not some old discarded pair bought from Raggy Mo at the market?

'Oh yer?' said Fowler.

His bogie eyes took in the boots. His nostrils flared, smelling the bacon hock simmering in the skilly pot over the fire. Since the collecting began, they had had bacon twice a week. And sugar in their tea. And marmady. Fowler's nose twitched like a lurcher's scenting game.

'You been to see that Pitford, then?' he said. He drew a handkerchief neatly pressed by his ma from his vest pocket and removed his hat. A band of sweat circled his forehead, leaving a mark like the crack around a boiled egg. He smelled rich and sweet, like fruit left too long to ferment in the sun. Summer made him irritable.

Allbones was nonchalant. 'Who?' he said. 'Oh, him. Yer.'

'Give you a rarkin'?' said Fowler, peering into the little window pane to straighten his collar.

'Somethin' like that,' said Allbones. On the table between them stood the little china jug Mary Anne had purchased with her shilling. Allbones had given them all a shilling to spend as they wished and she had spent hers on a jug ornamented with pink roses, which she had filled with daisies and speedwell. It shone in the dark cottage among the chipped plates and smoke-blackened timber. And Fowler's bogie eyes had taken in that too.

'So, what'd he say exactly?' he said.

'Mind my step, not take what isn't mine to take, the usual

cod,' said Allbones. 'Nothing serious. Just a warnin'. He had no evidence.'

'An' you cleared my 'name?' said Fowler, refolding the handkerchief and placing it in his pocket so that a triangular point protruded.

'Course,' said Allbones. 'You won't be hearin' any more from him.'

'You sure?' said Fowler.

'Certain,' said Allbones. He took a lace and began threading it through the eyelets on his new boot, slowly, unhurriedly. Fowler's body blocked the doorway like a sack over a rabbit hole. Sunlight squeezed around his edges.

'Nothin' else?' said Fowler. He had the handkerchief arranged to his satisfaction.

'He thanked me for showin' him the badgers,' said Allbones. 'I told you about that: the girl wanted to see the cubs.' Despite himself his fingers trembled slightly and the lace buckled and jammed.

'An' that was all?' said Fowler.

'Yer,' said Allbones. The lace was through. He bent down to put the boot on his foot. Fowler had him stopped up but there were still the stairs. He'd made a run for them often enough when his father was alive and back from the public house with a bit of hazel stick to knock them all into shape. Up the stairs and out the end window onto the sty roof next door. It was a steep drop and the window was small and it was years since he'd tried it, but there was something about this conversation that was not quite as Allbones would have wished: a watchful menace, the bogie eyes taking in all the detail and adding one and one to make two and a quarter. 'I'm tellin' you: you're out of trouble. All right?'

Fowler shifted his weight.

'Izzat so?' he said. 'Because I been hearin' talk.'

'Oh yer?' said Allbones, tugging the lace tight on stiff new leather. 'What kind of talk?'

'You been buyin' stock,' said Fowler.

'Just one or two,' said Allbones. 'Replacements. You know how it is, end of the season.'

'Not just one or two,' said Fowler. '*Quantities*. You been buyin' *quantities*.'

The barrel beside the door, within Fowler's reach, seethed with ferrets, all sluts, all dozing in a single mess, all bought from a ratcatcher past Tolby. All ready to join their co-emigrants early next Friday morning in the palatial cages by the aviary wall.

'Who says so?' said Allbones. 'One or two, that's all. A couple of breeders. Lost my white hob, din' I? Went missin' when my back was turned.'

But Fowler was not to be diverted by the white hob.

'My ma's sister says so,' he said conversationally. As if the two of them were settling in for an easy chat. 'Came visitin', din' she, last Sunday. And she told my ma she'd got rid of the last of her husband's stock. Nine ferrets. Old 'uns and young 'uns, the lot. To a skinny little runt with ginger hair, a baiter from over Netherton way. Called himself Smith. But I don't know any baiters called Smith.'

'Maybe he's new around here,' said Allbones.

'So I started askin' round,' said Fowler. 'An' it seems like this Smith or whatever he calls himself has been doin' a lot of buyin' lately. Payin' good money, too. An' it's always the same: skinny chap, ginger hair, with sovereigns. There's not a ferret to be had for ten miles round. Cleared out the county over the past month. All bought and paid for with nice new sovereigns. An' what I want to know is . . .' Fowler cleared his throat; this was a long speech for him, '. . . just how this little ginger runt came by so many sovereigns. Eh?'

Allbones had on his boots. He made a sudden dash for the stairs but Fowler was ready for him and, though large, he could move with surprising speed. He had him by one skinny ankle and held on with a mastiff's solid strength.

'Yer,' he said, breathing heavily. 'An' might there be some connection with a certain conversation with a certain gentleman about a month ago concerning — what was it now? Badgers. Yer. Fuckin' badgers . . .'

Allbones felt himself being drawn inexorably down, scraping and scrambling and saying he didn't know what Fowler was talking about, didn't have a clue and he was kicking hard but Fowler was too light-footed for that. He held on and, feet braced against a stair tread, drew down his quarry, nice and steady, in the direction of the hearth.

'I think you do know what I'm talkin' about,' Fowler said. 'I think you know *ezzackly*.'

And that was when he noticed the hock. The bacon hock, pink and juicy, in a pot filled with beans and barley. Transferring his grip so that Allbones was still held fast, he reached over and lifted the lid. 'Somethin' smells good,' he said, dabbling in the stew with one pudgy hand. 'Yer,' he said, drawing out the bone. 'Somethin' smells very good. But it ain't you, my lad.' He held Allbones fast and tore at the bone, dragging off a strip of pink meat.

'You want to know what I think?' he said, chewing contemplatively. 'I think you've come into some good fortune.' Fat dribbled down his puckered chin. 'An' I think it's somethin' to do with a certain conversation with a certain individual. Am I right?'

Allbones said nothing, concentrating all his effort on going limp and offering no resistance. As soon as the big man relaxed, he'd be off. Fowler gnawed off another chunk of bacon and gave him a little shake.

'An individual known as Pitford,' he said. Shake shake.

'No,' said Allbones.

'Liar,' said Fowler equably. He tossed the bone back in the pot. The embers glowed red and he used all his force to bend Allbones' face toward the heat. Closer. Closer. 'Bloody liar,' he said.

Allbones could smell the choking scent of singed hair. His face scorched. Passivity was going to get him nowhere. He began to squirm.

'It's true!' he said, hearing his voice become squeaky with fright.

'What'd you talk about, then?' said Fowler.

'I told you already!' said Allbones.

'Liar,' said Fowler.

Allbones' eyebrows fizzed and sizzled. He closed his eyes lest his eyeballs melt, and felt his mouth choking on gritty little puffs of ash raised by his frantic breathing, and still he was being pressed closer to the fire, closer . . .

'All righ'!' he said. 'All righ'! Pitford wanted some ferrets. An' he asked me to collect them for him. All righ'?'

The flames glowed crimson through his closed eyelids. He twisted and squirmed, fighting to get a leg free, to bring his foot up, shod in its new steel-toed boot. He bit and thrashed.

Fowler held on, unperturbed. 'How many?' he said.

'A hundred,' said Allbones.

'A hundred!' said Fowler. 'At two shillin's a head?'

'Yer!' said Allbones. Fowler shook him hard so that his head knocked in a *ratatat* of bruising blows against the sooty hearth.

''Ceptin' you're not bein' paid two shillin' a head, are you?' he said. 'You little twister. You're gettin' . . . what? Three shillin's a head? Three and sixpence?'

'I got expenses,' said Allbones frantically. 'Boots 'n that. It's been hard, all that travellin', on my boots.'

'Ah . . . yer . . .' said Fowler. 'Expenses . . .' There was a pause while he thought it through. Notion succeeded notion in a plodding progress through the jelly crevices of his brain. 'So . . .' he said at last, 'this Pitford asked you to collect a hundred ferrets for him?'

'Yer!' said Allbones.

'He asked you, Walter Allbones?' said Fowler.

Sweat was soaking Allbones' shoulders.

'Look, I din' want to go up there!' said Allbones. 'You made me!'

'To clear my name,' said Fowler. His voice became soft and more menacing. He tightened his grip, making a bouquet of Allbones' arms. 'You did clear my name, din' you? You did clear up any misunderstandin' like you said you would?'

A flame licked Allbones' cheek.

'Two things doth the Lord hate,' said Fowler. 'I'n that what the Book says? A proud look and a lyin' tongue. I'n that so, you little runt? A lyin' tongue. So — who did Pitford ask to collect his ferrets?'

'Metcalfe,' squealed Allbones, like a rabbit dragged from the burrow. 'He asked Fowler Metcalfe!'

Fowler was going to kill him. Inquisitor and executioner

both, his breathing was heavy as his full weight came down, pressing Allbones to the fire.

'Ahh,' he said. 'I thought so. Metcalfe. Not Allbones, but Metcalfe!' Allbones could smell his own skin and it smelled suspiciously like pork crackling.

'I'll make it right!' he squeaked. 'I will!'

Fowler settled himself on his stool. 'Indeed you will, my lad,' he said. And his grip slackened at last. 'Get up,' he said. 'An' don' you go runnin' off, because you an' me has got business to discuss, hasn' we?' Allbones backed away from the hearth, wincing at the burn on his cheek.

'What kind of business?' he said, dusting off ash and taking a wary seat on the third tread of the stairs.

'If it's Fowler Metcalfe who's collectin' ferrets,' said Fowler, 'then Fowler Metcalfe wants his share. That's only fair. Otherwise, he'll tell the truth.'

'The truth?' said Allbones.

Fowler leaned forward and lifted a piece of rind from the pot, holding it delicately and running it between his big square teeth.

'Yer,' he said. 'I go and see Pitford myself and I tell him he's been dealin' with the wrong man.'

His eyes were small and filled with calculation. Allbones thought rapidly, racing around the situation looking for a way out.

'You could do that,' he said. 'But I've met the man and he's not the kind to be mucked about. He's not a patient man. Why upset things? I've already got him a hundred. Plus the thirty there in the barrel to deliver this mornin'. Only a hundred more and we've finished!'

Fowler's bogie eyes swung into focus.

'Thirty?' he said. 'Another hundred? I thought you said you was collectin' a hundred total?'

'Two hundred and thirty,' said Allbones. 'An' that's God's truth.'

'Two hundred and thirty!' said Fowler. 'At what? Three shillin's a head?'

Allbones nodded. 'Two shillin's to the breeders, a shillin' clear.'

Fowler frowned as he made the calculations. He chewed on the rind. The room smelled of bacon and singed hair.

'Two pound,' said Allbones. 'I'll give you two pound and no talkin' and upsettin' Pitford.'

'Nah,' said Fowler.

'That's a quarter of my profit,' said Allbones.

'Nah,' said Fowler.

'Be reasonable,' said Allbones.

'Half,' said Fowler. 'We go halves.'

Allbones wriggled his toes in his new boots. The toe on the left boot pinched. The right boot was fine but the left promised to be awkward. He'd have blisters, rubbed raw. There was nothing for it but to wear them in, put up with the pain until the leather softened. He would walk carefully until the boots had moulded to the shape of his feet. Wasn't that always the way? Finding the knack of walking when one foot did not quite match the other. In time, they would reach a compromise. In time you would forget that there had ever even had to be a compromise.

Fowler spat on his hand. 'Halves it is,' he said.

Allbones had no option but to accept.

The big lad lumbered to his feet, cheerful again, forgiving, generous. 'Might even help with collectin' and deliverin', seein' it's my name on the stock. Keep an eye on you.' The little jug on the table toppled as he passed and fell to one side, spilling water and daisies. He lifted the lid on the barrel and lifted out one of the sandies.

'Not bad,' he said, examining her closely. 'What's he want 'em for?'

'Breedin',' said Allbones. 'And rabbits.' And as Fowler examined his stock he told him about these islands a great way off where the rabbits was undermining the houses and the folk had called in the army but they'd failed to solve the problem so now Pitford was sending ferrets and stoats and weasels to their aid . . .

So here they are: two young men walking along a road. One a gingery, twitching, darting lad, the other heavy and damp, his flesh rolling grandly as he moves. The road passes between hedgerows heavy with green summer leaf bordering fields where black and white cattle graze and the air is sweet with the scent of summer milk and soft grassy plops among the buttercups. Birds sing on every side and although it is early, the hay-makers are at work, moving steadily across the fields on the far side of the river. Through gaps in the hedges they can look down on men advancing on a rippling sea of fescue and timothy grass and the flash of sharpened blades as their scythes cut clean through the stalk, and behind them the small bent figures of the field workers stoop to gather armfuls of shorn grass into stooks. No one looks up to where two young men are taking the road out of the valley toward the edge and the blue sweep of the sky. The gingery man limps slightly, for he has a blister on the joint of his big toe, and besides, it is he who bears the heavier load. The day is already warm, yet he wears a thick overcoat and over one shoulder he carries a bulging sack. The heavy man carries just a couple of small wooden boxes. He swings along on curiously tiny feet, whistling.

'*He swings through the air*,' in duet with thrushes and blackbirds, '*with the greatest of ease . . .*' His bun hat perches on his bald head like a laurel wreath. He wears it as the victor, the champion, the clever fellow.

They come to the iron gates of a big house. As they pass through into the stableyard, the gingery one says, 'You're to say nothin', mind. Just leave me to do the talkin'.' And the other says, 'Won' say a word, but I'll be listenin' hard.'

Donnithorne stood as usual, mournfully screwing a catch onto another cage. The aviary wall was now stacked four deep with cages stretching from one side of the yard to the other, and the rank smell of confined mustelids overwhelmed the scent of freshly sawn timber. One of the lads was engaged in feeding them, picking scraps of scraggy mutton from a bucket and dropping them gingerly through the traps.

Donnithorne eyed the sack with distaste.

'So you've brought us more of they stinkin' beasts,' he said.

'I have,' said Allbones, setting his load down on the cobbles with relief. 'Twenty-two ferrets and eight stoats. Good 'uns too.'

'When we're short-staffed an' all,' said Donnithorne. 'Arthur's off sick so Victor here's managin' the feedin' on 'is own, and a right performance he's makin' of it, too.'

The lad flushed, his ears flaring like two crimson petals either side of his closely shaven skull.

'S'not easy,' he said, wiping his nose with a bloody hand. 'They're right picky. They're not eatin'. Gone off their food.' His voice was hoarse, his eyes red-rimmed.

'An' he's not well hisself,' said Donnithorne.

'Nowt but a summer cold,' said the lad, then sneezed mightily.

'Off their food?' said Allbones.

'Yer,' said the lad. 'It's fresh meat, like you said. But they're just sittin' there, turnin' up their noses.'

Allbones peered into one of the cages. A sandie hunched in a corner, its bedding matted with scraps of stale meat. He picked it up. It was shivering and its soft body was hot to the touch. He tipped it on its back. No red patching, thank God, no sprinkle of telltale red dots about the lips, and the feet were not swollen. Not distemper. The ferret sprawled listless on his palm, then stiffened in a tiny spasm. Achoo. Achoo.

'How many are off their food, would you say?' he said.

The lad shrugged.

'Dunno,' he said. 'A few.'

Allbones replaced the sick ferret and rapidly inspected the other cages. In some, the inhabitants slept or chewed happily, but in one, two, a dozen, two dozen, the animals huddled in fever. He turned on the lad in fury.

'Idiot!' he yelled. 'You fuckin' bessy! They takes the influenza! Just like us! They gets a fever, they sneeze, they goes off their food an' then, like as not, they'll catch pneumonie and then they'll die! What was you thinkin' of, to tend 'em when you're ill?'

The lad flushed again, defensive.

'I din' know that, did I?' he said. 'Mr Donnithorne said to feed 'em, so I fed 'em! I din' want to feed 'em. I hates the little

111

buggers. But 'e asked me, so I did!'

Donnithorne drooped, his shoulders sagging before the inevitability of fate, the certainty that everything he did or suggested was bound to lead to disaster.

'Isn' that the way?' he said. 'All your collectin' for nowt! They's all goin' to die an' all our effort's been wasted.' He sighed heavily. 'You can tell Mr Pitford the sad news yourself when you sees him. He wants to talk to you. He's in that there avery, lookin' at his birds.'

He accompanied them to the gate: Allbones and Fowler who kept close, heavy and watchful, to Allbones' shoulder. Pitford was standing observing a large green parrot that hung upside down from the wire netting, making its own observations of humanity with its black button eyes before the image of snow-topped mountains.

'Ah, Metcalfe!' he said, and Allbones could hear Fowler's hiss. He was indeed listening hard. 'So you have delivered another consignment!'

'Yes sir,' said Allbones.

''Cept they're all goin' to die, sir,' said Donnithorne. 'That's what Mr Metcalfe here has been tellin' us. They're off their vittles, caught the influenza from Victor an' in a day or so they'll be dead.' He took some grim satisfaction in the prospect. 'Yes. Dead and gone.' A hundred and thirty little corpses, laid out, row on row.

Pitford turned to Allbones in alarm.

'Is this so?' he said.

'Well, there's some with influenza,' said Allbones. 'No doubt about that. They shouldn' ever be tended by someone who's ill. But they won' die, not if they're kept warm and well fed an' watered.'

'An' if they live,' said Fowler, unable to hover a moment longer in the background, 'they'll be stronger 'n ever. Never take the sniffles again. So it's not all bad, sir.'

'Indeed?' said Pitford, taking in the new arrival. 'And to whom do I owe this reassurance?'

Allbones took a deep breath.

'This is Allbones, sir,' he said. 'Walter Allbones. I might have mentioned him some weeks ago.'

'The breeder of superior ferrets!' said Pitford. 'Ah yes, Mr Allbones. Delighted to make your acquaintance! Metcalfe here speaks most highly of you. In fact, he deferred to your superior knowledge and experience!'

'Did he now?' said Fowler, bogie eyes swivelling in separate trajectories in a fashion that did not bode well for the journey back to the Bottom End.

'Indeed he did,' said Pitford. 'He said your stock was the best in the county.'

The eyes bulged.

'Walter's offered to help,' said Allbones rapidly. 'With the collectin', now that we're havin' to spread the net wider, like. We're splittin' the difference.'

Pitford nodded in approval.

'Excellent,' he said. 'Two experts where previously we had one. You have heard their opinion, Donnithorne: now you must go and act upon it!'

Donnithorne shuffled off to relieve Victor of his duties, muttering under his breath at the nuisance of having to lay his own work aside to feed the stinking beasts himself: it wasn't what he was employed for, not a skilled carpenter like himself ... The gate clicked shut behind his doleful back.

'Which brings me,' said Pitford, 'to the matter I wished

to discuss this morning. Clearly, the task of caring for so many animals is becoming demanding. If they are to be kept in the best of health, they will need skilled attention. What would you say, Metcalfe, to regular employment as ferret keeper? Seven days a week for their feeding and care? I should make it worth your while. Five shillings a day? Would that be acceptable?'

Allbones kept his eyes fixed on the toes of his new boots. 'Well, yes, sir,' he said. 'Most acceptable.'

He could hear Fowler breathing stertorously at his shoulder.

'Starting immediately, since the lad has the plague,' said Pitford. 'For five weeks until transportation. And beyond . . .'

'Beyond?' said Allbones.

'Yes, Metcalfe,' said Pitford. 'Beyond, for they must be cared for here, but also during the voyage if they are to arrive safely at their destination.'

'On them islands?' said Allbones.

'Yes,' said Pitford. 'New Zealand. Experience over the past few years has proved that collecting the animals is a relatively straightforward matter. It is their transport that is fraught with difficulty. There have been several attempts to transport mustelids to the colony. Only a year ago a shipment of more than a thousand failed, despite their exporter's greatest care. He supplied them with fresh pigeon meat and spared no expense on their housing, but fewer than a quarter survived the voyage. The cause was in part that the exporter had transported them on an iron ship rather than a wooden one. And iron ships have proved unkind to livestock in the tropics, for they act like ovens. But even on wood, the odds of survival are not good: the creatures must spend many weeks at sea, they must cross some of the most tempestuous oceans on the planet, they must endure equatorial heat and Antarctic cold. To stand a chance of arriving safely in the colony, they will require the care of a highly skilled keeper. A lad like yourself, Metcalfe. What would you say to a voyage to the Antipodes?'

'I don't think so, sir,' said Allbones.

'Forty pounds, plus a bonus for every animal that arrives safe at its destination,' said Pitford.

Forty pounds!

'Five shillings for every weasel,' said Pitford. 'Seven shillings for every stoat and ferret. And your ticket home at the end of it. Now what do you say to that?'

A fortune. A windfall. It hung there before him, glittering. A swarm of golden sovereigns. But not his to take. Journey who knew where, over the wide ocean he had glimpsed once from behind his mother's skirts on a long-ago Saturday outing? Besides, who would care for the littl'uns while he was gone? They had kept the family from the workhouse thus far, he with his labouring, Mary Anne with her housewifery. She was capable enough, but it was too great a responsibility to handle alone. The sovereigns faded, turned to dust, to powder and blew away over the fields and woods that had always marked the borders of his life.

He stuttered. It was a generous offer . . . he would like to accept . . . but obligations . . .

'You would be abroad for some time, of course,' said Pitford. 'Four months out, a couple of months perhaps to see something of the country — and there are sights to see, believe me: mountains to rival Switzerland, volcanoes to equal Vesuvius, geysers and boiling mud, a flora and fauna unmatched for its curiosity — then four months to return home.'

'A long time, sir . . .' said Allbones. 'I don' think I could . . .'

Pitford interrupted him. 'You need to think it over. I understand that. It is an unexpected offer, though it has not been made lightly. I have great confidence in your skills, Metcalfe. Take a week to consider. And let me know your decision next Friday. Good day to you.'

They had been dismissed.

'What were you thinking of, man?' said Fowler as they walked back to the Bottom End, the day's tally of ferrets stowed in their cages, every one of them fed and watered and warmly bedded down, and those that ailed securely quarantined within the shelter of the workshop. He swung a hazel stick broken from the hedge as he walked.

'Forty pound!' A thistlehead was knocked clean into the air. 'Mr fuckin' Metcalfe!'

'You could see how he is,' said Allbones. ('Hello! Hello!' the bird had cried, but of Eugenia herself there had been no sign. Not even a wraith at an upstairs window, though he had glanced up often enough as they worked in the stableyard. Now the empty sack sagged on his shoulders. His coat was too heavy, too hot. Its weight was smothering.) 'You could see he's not the type you'd want to upset. And it's only a few weeks till we're done with collectin'. It won' make no difference.'

Fowler stopped dead in the middle of the road. 'A few weeks!' he said.

'Yer,' said Allbones.

'I thought we'd finished,' said Fowler. 'You said two hundred and thirty. That's what you said.'

'Three hundred and fifty,' said Allbones wearily. 'He

wants three hundred and fifty or thereabouts.'

'You sure?' said Fowler. 'You little liar. You little twister. Three hundred an' fifty? That's all? Not four hundred, maybe?'

'No,' said Allbones.

'Or a thousand, like the man said? A thousand ferrets?' persisted Fowler.

'Three hundred and fifty,' said Allbones. He didn't care if Fowler threw him to the ground or started to rage. She had not been there, as she had not been there ever since she ran from the room that afternoon when she had shown him her pictures. She had vanished into the maze of corridors in the great house like a small animal gone to ground. 'A hundred and some, and we're done. An' we'll go halves, like you said. A few weeks' work caring for them then it's all over and you can go back to being Fowler Metcalfe again. And I can be Walter fuckin' Allbones.'

'So you're not takin' the forty pounds?' said Fowler in amazement.

''Course not,' said Allbones.

'You don' plan on goin' to them islands?'

'No,' said Allbones. 'Don' be daft. Why should I want to go there?'

'I'd like to go,' said Fowler. 'I seen this girl once at Brinkton Fair: this tinker had a box you could look in for a penny and there was this girl on an island. She were all dark, you know, from livin' on this island where the sun's shinin' all year long and she was right pretty: no boots, just her bare feet, but wearin' a dress — respectable like. You'd take her for English if it weren't for her bein' black as your hat. An' then the tinkerman said if I gave him another penny, I'd see somethin' to make my eyes pop, an' so I said why not? An' he turned this little handle thing on the side of the box and blow me, but this girl started takin' all her clothes off: skirt and jacket an' then he said if I gave him another penny, she'd be as Adam saw her. An' so I did, an' she were down to nothin' at all. She were from one of them islands. Other side of the world, that's what the tinker said. An' I've wanted to go out there ever since.'

'Not me,' said Allbones.

'Why not?' said Fowler. His face was creased with puzzlement. 'She were right pretty an' all.'

'I like it well enough here,' said Allbones. A summer day, a bacon hock for his dinner in the pot on the fire. Across the river, the hay-makers were still at work, the tall grasses driven back to a small redoubt at the very centre of the field. The field workers bent to their toil in a shimmery haze of dust and afternoon heat. While he, Allbones, had money in his pocket for little effort. Not Allbones, but No-bones.

'You like it better than forty pound an' a place with boilin' mud where the girls go about bare as a bird's bum?' said Fowler.

'Yes,' said Allbones.

Fowler straightened his little bun hat. 'Then you're daft,' he said, and he strode off down the road, leaving a harvest of slaughtered thistles in his wake, while Allbones trailed homeward with an empty heart.

5.

The Robin (pitoitoi) is seldom met with on the mainland, and, in common with many other native forms, its doom is sealed. Ornithologists everywhere must regret this, because the genus to which it belongs has no representative in any other part of the world: and those who are at all familiar with the bird itself will assuredly grieve over its threatened extirpation.

Personally I regard this gentle Robin with a strong sentiment of affection. In the days of my boyhood it was one of the dominant species and some of my earliest memories are associated with it. The first nest I ever found in my juvenile excursions through the bush near the parental home — the dear old Church Mission station of forty years ago — was naturally that of the Robin. It was the first bird of which I ever prepared a specimen . . . Ere long the bird itself

will be but a memory of by-gone years. Either
on account of its being an easy prey to wild cats
and rats, or else in obedience to some
inescapable law of nature, the species is rapidly
dying out: and it requires no prophetic vision to
foresee its utter extinction within a very short
period. Well may the Maori say, as he laments
over the decadence of his own race — 'Even as
the Pitoitoi has vanished from the woods, so
will the Maori pass away from the land and be
forgotten!'

Walter Buller, A History of the Birds of New Zealand

There was a flutter of white at the very edge of the trees where their dark shadow marked the boundary to a golden swathe of summer grass. Allbones straightened carefully from resetting the trap, one young weasel already caught and squealing in the carrybox. They were the most difficult to catch, but over the past months he had refined his technique until he had it perfect: a chicken's egg set temptingly in a length of pipe along with a cunning and delicate arrangement of tripwire and drop. It took time to set, but it was worth it for the skill it took. He had taken weasels by the river, in Ledney Wood, and even here, within the walls on land that until now had been prohibited to him. He moved about here now with impunity, setting his traps in broad daylight with the owner's express approval. It gave him a fine confidence that he no longer had to skulk and hide. He had not so far encountered any groundsmen but he found himself choosing the middle of the day for his work, hoping almost to be intercepted. How he would face the challenge down, say carelessly, 'I'm employed by Mr Pitford.' As he set his traps he found himself rehearsing the scene in his mind's eye: the other man backing off, apologising. The thought gave him deep satisfaction.

The fluttering, like a white wing, caught his eye.

She was moving erratically across the grass in a light summer dress, sometimes in sunlight, sometimes darting sideways into the shadow of the trees. In one hand she held a long pole with a white net. It waved like a flag above grass bowed over with seed, waved this way and that as she pursued the invisible. Over one shoulder she carried a square satchel and from time to time she stopped altogether, took something from it, held it to the light, replaced it.

Allbones shrank down into the cover of bramble and periwinkle beneath the trees to watch. She was absorbed, flitting about the way swallows fly over water in the long summer twilight, when midges in their jittery leks are dancing out their one day of existence. He wriggled forward and parted the grass to see her more clearly. The midday sun caught her hair hanging loose under a straw hat, and when she entered the shade of the trees her dress became dappled. Out again she came, waving her white net. It dipped and swayed and twisted. She came closer and he could see her face, flushed with effort, her brow furrowed in concentration. Her eyes were shadowed beneath the brim of her hat, from which a blue ribbon flew in the lightest of breezes. The grass reached to her waist so she sailed toward him in her white dress. He could hear the slight 'oof' as she reached and missed and swept and danced to the left, to the right.

She did not see him there crouched in the undergrowth. Suddenly he felt a little ridiculous. He should have left before this, wriggled off into the shadows as soon as she appeared instead of lying there watching. Now it was too late. She had stopped only a few yards away by a fallen log. She propped net and satchel against it and sat down. Allbones held his breath. He watched as she bent down and lifted her skirt. Muslin, white cotton petticoats, a froth of lace edging. She unrolled one stocking, her foot raised in the air. She wriggled her bare toes. He was close enough to glimpse the pale skin of her thigh, the red mark where the garter had pressed into her flesh, the boney knob of her knee, the curve of her calf, her slender ankle and little wriggling toes. She tugged off the other stocking, rolled them both in a ball and stuffed them into her satchel. She took out a bottle and tipped her head back and drank deeply. He could hear the gulp of water in her throat.

He was trapped in a green tunnel. A thorny twig pressed uncomfortably against his forehead, and one leg, bent beneath him, was becoming cramped. He wanted desperately to move, but had to crouch, frozen, while she sat in the sunlight, unhurriedly taking a jar from the satchel, into which she peered. She gave it a little shake and set it down on the log beside her. She removed her hat, lifted her hair away from the back of her neck and twisted it roughly into a knot on top of her head. She sighed deeply and raised her face to the sun, eyes shut.

Allbones' leg was completely numb. He pinched it and could feel no sensation whatsoever. He tried to ease his weight but at the slightest movement the crackling of dry twigs sounded deafening. Now she was looking up. She was picking up her net; she was getting to her feet. A dragonfly hovered on its twin wings a little to her left. Cautiously she raised the net. It flew suddenly to the right, then straight toward the trees. She followed it. It shifted direction and now it was coming directly toward Allbones. He could see it passing through dappled shade, its body shimmering blue and green, and then it came to a halt the way they do, wings whirring busily right above the spot where Allbones crouched on cramped legs. She stood not two yards off, the net raised, and suddenly, as she made the sweep, she saw him there.

'Oh!' she said. 'Oh my goodness!' The net fell. The dragonfly sprang into motion, zigzagging off toward the place where the stream had formed a pond behind fallen branches, dark and silent in the green woods.

Allbones scrambled to his feet, stumbling as his left leg fought for sensation.

'Afternoon, Miss,' he said, and knew he sounded ridiculous, looked ridiculous with twigs sticking to his hair and to his muddy trousers. He held up the box that contained the weasel. 'I bin trappin',' he said. 'Din' mean to startle you, like.'

Eugenia picked up her net. 'You didn't,' she said. 'At least, you did for just a second. And you made me miss my specimen. It was a good one, too. *Cordulegaster annulatus*.'

'You chasin' dragonflies?' said Allbones. It seemed necessary to make a conversation, to establish normality, despite the twigs and his peculiar emergence from the undergrowth.

'Amongst other things,' said Eugenia. 'Look.' And she ran back to the log to retrieve the jar. It held some laurel leaves and the bodies of several insects. 'A lacewing,' she said. 'That green one there, with the shiny eyes — and the cranefly, of course, and that, I think, might be *Calopteryx virgo*, the demoiselle Maiden dragonfly. I hope so, for I don't have one in my collection. I shall have to look it up.'

Her bare arms had a sprinkling of fair hairs. He could see the tracery of veins blue beneath the skin at the pit of the elbow and in the turn of her wrist. The insects lay still, tiny jointed legs raised in the air and crisscrossed, like the legs of the knight on the tomb in Ledney Church. He peered through the glass at their wings refracting scarlet, blue and green, their tiny armoured bodies, their bulbous eyes set like jet beads.

'They're right pretty,' said Allbones. She was a girl, after all. Of course she would collect what was pretty and colourful, just as Mary Anne spent her shilling on a cream jug painted with roses.

Eugenia sniffed. 'I don't collect them because they're pretty,' she said. 'I collect them because they interest me. Especially the Odonata — that's dragonflies,' she added helpfully. 'I already own one hundred and eighty specimens representing thirty-seven species.'

'What do you do with them all?' said Allbones.

'I mount them on cards,' said Eugenia. 'It's very exacting. They must be pinned first onto corked board with their wings and legs spread out on either side just so. Some species have to be stuffed with cottonwool, and that is really fiddly work. But I'm very good at it. Small fingers, you see.'

She held up a hand — small, white. Like a bird's claw. Like a kitten's paw.

'And when they're dry I pin them onto cards and label them properly, then put them into my cabinet.'

'Like them birds up in the house,' said Allbones. 'The ones in the drawers?'

'Exactly,' said Eugenia.

'It does seem a shame, all this collectin', when they might be off flyin' about the fields and woods,' said Allbones.

'They don't suffer,' said Eugenia. 'The laurel vapour kills them instantly. And it is not done out of cruelty, but for science. How else are we to understand the natural world? And you collect, too,' she added a trifle defensively. 'You have your ferrets. Do you collect them because they're "pretty"?'

She made the word ridiculous.

'They're useful,' said Allbones. 'They kill rats.' He paused. He had never thought before about why he kept ferrets. Other lads in the village had pigeons or fowls or kept no animals at all, preferring to spend their leisure time fishing or kicking a ball about or squabbling over penny toss. This girl asked such odd questions yet he felt compelled to fumble for an answer. 'An' I like 'em, I suppose. I could use a dog for ratting, a terrier — but I prefer the ferrets. I like their faces, the way they stare at you, straight and unafeared. Like, they don't care what we think, not the way a dog cares. A dog is always hangin' on your every move, worrying that he's not understood you right, but a ferret don' care. No matter how long you own one, it's still wild in its heart, it'll still take a bite at you if you disturb it. It's its own master. It fears nothing. It'll take on a rabbit or a rat or a hen ten times its size, an' it'll win. An' I like their paws, the way they folds 'em when they're sleepin' an' the way they holds their food up to eat like they was proper hands. They're bold and they're quick to learn an' they're soft when you carry 'em. An' yes, they're pretty creatures.'

It was the longest speech he had ever made in his life. Eugenia stood before him in the sunlight, her head tilted a little as she listened. And as he spoke he felt his hand reach out and touch her. He ran the back of one finger along the curve of her jaw.

'Like you,' he said.

Her skin was softer than he had ever imagined — cool and smooth, like something valuable: china, rimmed with gold.

'You said that before,' she said. 'That I was beautiful.'

'You are,' said Allbones. The words cracked as they forced their way past the constriction in his throat. 'Your hair . . .' At last he touched her hair. A strand curled around his finger the way a tendril attaches itself to a twig. 'Your face . . .' Curve of brow and cheek, her breath on the palm of his hand. Her lips like the petals of some flower: a buttercup, perhaps, when it has just broken from the bud on a spring morning when everything is sleek and fresh. He kissed her. She tasted of sunshine and dry grass and soap and violets.

She stood clasping her satchel so that its edges pressed uncomfortably between them. He drew back. Her eyes were open and observing him keenly.

'What a curious sensation,' she said. 'Your mouth on mine.'

'Did you like it?' he said.

She considered the question. 'Yes,' she said. 'I think so. I'm not sure.'

'Have you ever been kissed before?' he said. (He had: as prelude to a boozy wet-lipped fumbling with Lardy Annie in the alleyway behind the King's Arms one fair night. She'd asked him for a shilling first, to buy herself some stockings. And before that, there had been a girl who had arrived with her family one Easter and taken up residence in the rundown cottage behind the church. Her father was a labourer, her mother a loud, clanging woman who had the knack of making other women laugh, though there were some who avoided her for being common. For six months laughter blew without restraint from behind the rackety door, the kind of laughter that stopped the instant husband or child drew near. Sally took after her father, being sullen and not given to conversation, but Allbones kissed her twice in Ledney Wood before the family up and left overnight, all their possessions piled on a barrow and two weeks' rent in arrears. Sally had returned his kiss perfunctorily. Her hair was matted and smelled of tallow candles and her mouth was smeared with blackberry juice. She had accepted his advances as a hen does when the rooster seizes her by the neck and mounts her, as something to be tolerated for a minute or so until it's over and she can return to dusting her wings and settling her feathers. 'Give over, do!' she had said. And returned to picking blackberries.)

This was different. Eugenia considered his question with the same seriousness she devoted to all enquiry.

'Have I been kissed?' she said. 'No, at least not like that. My mother kissed me when I was small, when I lived in India. And my father. And my amah, of course. And my grandfather . . . But . . . this was different . . .' She paused. 'You may do it again if you like.'

This time she lowered the satchel and Allbones, leaning closer, could feel the softness of small breasts and the jut of her hips through layers of muslin and cotton when he placed his hands about her waist. Her lips beneath his own had parted. He could feel the press of her teeth and there was no sound other than the rush of his own blood surging. His breathing quickened. She drew away. Allbones felt himself chastened and suddenly awkward.

'Sorry,' he said. 'I hope I haven't given offence.'

But she was not offended at all.

'I liked it,' she said, and this time she reached up and placed her lips on his.

In the dark tunnels of his body his blood began to sing. Around them the summer creatures buzzed in the long grass and a breeze ruffled the leafy wood and he was placing his arms about her and he was kissing her forehead, her cheeks, her lips, her nose. And she was kissing him. Delicately, as if she were tasting him. His mouth. His chin. His forehead. As if this were some experiment requiring exquisite judgement. Waist deep in summer grass they stood face to face. Fieldmice rustled through dry stalks, and a million tiny creatures darted about, meeting, coupling, dying, while pigeons called from the wood, their cooing rhythmic as a cradle rocking back and forth, back and forth on a bare wooden floor.

A fly had landed on her hair. At such close quarters he could see its bulbous eyes shining as if they were made of golden metal and its armoured body shimmering indigo and its tiny jointed legs. Usually he would have flicked it aside, or killed it, but everything at this moment seemed perfect, as if it belonged here and had a right to live its life in whatever manner it chose. It was cleaning itself, rubbing its head with its legs like a small black kitten cleaning behind its ears, then polishing its wings until they gleamed an exquisite iridescent blue. Allbones had never looked at an insect so closely before. Flies were simply a nuisance, pests that tainted and spoiled, their armoured legions infiltrating seething maggoty hordes into meat and cheese. For the first time, though, he saw that a fly was exquisite. He caught it between his fingers.

'Here,' he said to Eugenia. 'Mebbe this'll do instead of that dragonfly you was after.'

The fly buzzed in panic, its tiny dancer's legs fighting.

'Linnaeus said three of these could consume the carcass of a horse as efficiently as a lion: five thousand six hunded million progeny in a month,' she said. 'But I have one already. *Lonchaea chorea*. They're common and easy to catch.'

She flicked it from his hand. 'Whereas the ringed club is terribly difficult. They have huge eyes and can see in every direction.'

She sighed.

'I shall never complete my collection before we leave,' she said.

The word had a flat click to it, like a door closing on an empty room.

'You're leavin'?' he said. 'Where are you goin'?'

'Why, to New Zealand, of course,' said Eugenia.

'That place my ferrets is to rescue?' said Allbones.

'Yes,' said Eugenia.

'Why ever would you want to go there?' said Allbones. 'All those thousands of miles away?'

'My grandfather has decided we should go after all,' she said. 'He is a scientist so of course he wishes to visit his laboratory. He will ensure the ferrets are safely delivered and oversee the care of the birds on the return voyage. They are too valuable to be entrusted to some ignorant keeper.'

She picked at a grass stalk stuck to her skirt.

'And I am to accompany him. He thinks it would assist my education and that the sea voyage would benefit my health.'

'How long will you be away?' said Allbones.

'A year,' said Eugenia. 'Maybe longer. It would be absurd to travel so far and not spend time seeing the country. Do you not also plan to stay on for a time?'

'Well, I . . .' said Allbones.

'After you have seen the ferrets to their new home?' she said. When Allbones hesitated, she looked puzzled. 'You are coming, aren't you?' She looked at him with such expectation that Allbones found himself saying yes, of course he was going to be voyaging to New Zealand.

Eugenia smiled. 'It will be the most wonderful adventure,' she said. 'I wouldn't miss it for the world. I'm glad you will be there too.' And she touched his face, resting her hand lightly on his cheek.

There was a humming in the air behind his head, whirr and glitter between grass and the blue bowl of the sky.

Eugenia reached for her net. 'There he is again,' she whispered. 'The ringed club. So I haven't missed him after all.' The membrane of sunlight that had bound them body to body, face to face in the long grass, stretched and tore. The world broke through and the dragonfly darted off toward the pond among the trees, with Eugenia in pursuit. But just as the shadows took her she turned, net raised and, whispering so as not to disturb the creature zigzagging toward its doom in the killing jar, she said, 'Oh — and thank you. For the kiss.'

Politely. As if he had just handed her a posy.

Everything had changed.

'Of course you must go,' said Mary Anne, seated at the kitchen table in her new print dress. She tapped the teapot with a spoon and turned it three times to settle the leaf. 'It is a great opportunity.'

Willie Mossop sat awkwardly opposite, hair combed flat and collar uncomfortably buttoned to the neck and his big labourer's hands scrubbed to the callouses as he fumbled with a plate and a slice of sultana cake. He had called by with a dozen eggs in a basket, as he did most Sunday afternoons these days, bearing gifts: broad beans, a fowl all plucked and ready for the pot. Mary Anne for her part had taken to baking, turning out the cakes she had learned to make in service. The kitchen table was covered with a cloth she had embroidered with daisies and set with the plates and cups and saucers she had bought to accompany the elegance of the china cream jug. Willie Mossop watched her with undisguised admiration as she served the tea and asked would he care for another slice?

She added milk to his cup, just a drop, the way she knew he liked it, and said that she would manage. Walter would be earning good money, and while he was away earning it, if she needed a man to shift something or do the heavy work, well, Willie would help, wouldn't he? Willie nodded so vigorously that the teacup balanced precariously in his meaty paws rattled and slopped.

'Don' you worry, Walter,' he said. 'Don' you fret. You go off on that boat an' I'll see them're all taken care of. You have my word on it.'

He was a good man, older than Mary Anne by more than a decade, but kind and steady. After tea he would sit a while and smoke his pipe while she did the darning and both of them comfortable, talking of this and that, and it was clearly only a matter of time before he would be sitting across from Mary Anne to have his tea every night of the week.

But when Allbones knocked at Pitford's study door, hat in hand, to stand upon the Turkish rug and announce that he had reached his decision and would like to go to New Zealand, it appeared that he had been forestalled.

'But I have already appointed Mr Allbones,' said Pitford, a little irritably, thumping the blotter firmly onto a page of words run close like the marks of birds' feet over snow. 'I was assured that you had arranged it all between you and since he came with your highest recommendation, I thought it a most satisfactory arrangement.'

He picked up a pen and examined the nib.

'A place might be made for you as his assistant, perhaps,' he said. 'There will certainly be more than enough to keep the two of you occupied during the voyage. I could not pay you as much as I am paying Allbones, but . . .'

Ten pound, a return ticket, third class . . .

Behind Pitford's chair stood the table with its arrangement of crows, the male with its blunt beak equipped to hack at dead wood, the female with her slender scimitar. Pinned to the dais was a sheet of paper bearing an outline in black crayon, the work of a small white hand. Allbones swallowed hard and accepted Pitford's terms.

He found Fowler later, mucking out cages in the stable-yard.

'What do you mean, takin' the post he offered me?' Allbones said, and now it was his turn to go on the attack, but Fowler was unperturbed. He dumped a load of fouled straw into the barrow.

'You din' want to go!' he said. 'You said you was happy spendin' the rest of your days in Bottom End. That's what you said.'

'Well, I changed my mind,' said Allbones.

'Too late,' said Fowler. 'Should've taken it when it was yours for the askin'. Anyway, the job was Fowler Metcalfe's to begin with and now it is in truth. Don' worry. I won' tell. I'm Allbones. You're Metcalfe, till this job's over. It don' worry me much one way or t'other.' He upturned the barrow onto the midden heap. 'Told you you was a fool.'

'Well, I'm comin' too,' said Allbones. 'As your assistant.'

Fowler shrugged.

'Suit yourself,' he said. 'But you does ezzackly what I tells you an' the forty quid's all mine. Understand?'

Allbones understood.

6.

*Of every clean beast shalt thou take to thee by
sevens, the male and his female, and of beasts
that are not clean by two, the male and his
female. Of fowls also of the air by sevens, the
male and the female: to keep seed alive upon
the face of all the earth . . . And God blessed
Noah and his sons and said unto them, Be
fruitful and multiply and replenish the earth.
And the fear of you and the dread of you shall
be upon every beast of the earth and upon every
fowl of the air, upon all that moveth upon the
earth and upon all the fishes of the sea. Into
your hand are they delivered.*

Genesis, 7: 2–3; 9: 1–2

Allbones travelled south perched on a crate in a cattle wagon,
watching through the vent as England rushed backward at
eighty miles an hour. Trees and hedges tossed dry leaf already

tinted yellow and ruby red, and the countryside was revealed through billowing engine smoke that streamed and spun like a conjuror's curtain, now you see it now you don't, disclosing a farmhouse in a cluster of barn and pig pen or a little village where the pale stone of his native place had been displaced by brick and slate.

Rivers wound deep and slow among willow and wide fields of golden stubble, combed flat and burning. From his place of ease on the crate Allbones could see the blackened acres and the lines of flame like the tide rising over sand. Smoke billowed, making a crimson disc of the sun, and smuts blew in through the vent so that Allbones was forced to close his eyes, to smell his way south: the rasp of burnt grass and charred earth, the sweet ferment of apples fallen to damp orchard grass, the perfume of dung heaps piled high in muddy yards, the cheesy tang of cows browsing in the damp shade at a river's bend. And then the train entered some town and there were the acrid smells of foundry metal or brewers' vat blended with the press of horses, cabs and people in narrow houses on narrow streets, and there were stations where engine smoke billowed beneath high ceilings of bleary glass and more people than Allbones had ever seen gathered in one place milled about looking for their seats in first, second or third or joined the press about the buffet for their tea and penny buns.

Nose pressed to the vent, Allbones smelled his way away from home. The wagon itself supplied its own rich notes of dry cow dung and grassy sheep piss, and, overlying them all now, the panicky stink of frightened ferrets, alarmed by the noise and the unfamiliar jolts and clanging. His ferrets, stoats and weasels. Three hundred and fifty, as ordered, in cages stacked ten deep. The air within the wagon was reassuringly fetid.

In the carriage ahead, Fowler took up his share and more of a third-class bench, jostling for elbow room with a superior young lawyer's clerk who read his paper with a fine disregard for the passing scene beyond the grimy window, now you see it now you don't.

'This is more like it, innit?' Fowler had said as they had climbed aboard, their farewells all done, the familiar figures waving from the platform dwindling to a blur then vanishing altogether as the world gathered speed, and Ledney Wood, Brinkton, Tolby, the whole known universe dwindled and vanished, displaced by other woods and other villages, ones whose names they did not know. Allbones, wedged tightly in a corner, had watched the sober hedgerows begin to run, racing the train, rising and falling while Fowler attempted to engage the attention of a young serving girl on her way to a place in the city. She clung to a large velour bag as if it would keep her from ruin and kept her eyes on the scene beyond the window, clearly having been warned against the terrors of the great world beyond the farmstead where she had been born and raised. Fowler in new jacket, new boots and shiny bowler persisted nevertheless, delighting in his new role as man of the world, adventurer and roué.

'You're going to cross the ocean?' she said, her eyes wide with horror. 'Ooh, I could never do that! Never! I'd be afeared!'

Fowler had smiled reassuringly. 'Nothing to be frightened of,' he said. 'The ships are built here of good iron and British timber.' But the girl was telling him about this family from her aunt's village who had set off for Australia or one of them places only the year before and been all wrecked for a great boat had steamed right into them before they'd been gone a day, cut their ship in half like it was a pat of butter.

Allbones had listened as the girl, big spaniel eyes wide with the drama of it all, told her terrible story. 'So,' he said, unable to resist the enquiry, 'was they all drowned?'

'Course not,' said Fowler. 'They has lifeboats an' all, for an emergency.'

'They was saved,' said the girl, 'but they lost everything they owned. Clothes and furnishings and all. They was left with nothing but the clothes they stood up in. Eight minutes.' She nodded darkly. 'That was all it took from when the steamer hit them till their boat was sunk beneath the waves. There was a picture of it in the paper. The boat tipped over and all the people drifting on the ocean.' She settled the velour bag more securely on her knee. 'No,' she said, 'you wouldn't catch me on one of them boats. Not for all the tea in China.'

Fowler refused to be disconcerted. 'Poor seamanship,' he said, suddenly the expert on all things nautical. 'If someone had been taking proper notice, nothing like that would have happened.'

At that, the lawyer's clerk had intervened. The young lady was quite right to be cautious. He proceeded to regale the carriage with tales of other ships: ships that had set off in high hopes from London docks only to disappear mysteriously, presumably having borne their cargo of hapless emigrants to a watery grave; ships that had run aground in storms when only a few miles from their destination, whose passengers had drowned or been crushed on sharp reefs; ships that had caught fire mid-ocean and burned to their waterline, and the lifeboats that had escaped the conflagration drifted for days, the survivors dying one by one from thirst or engaging in dreadful cannibalistic orgies before eventual rescue. Comprehensively informed by his reading of the daily papers, he was a veritable encyclopedia of maritime disaster.

The young woman listened in appalled fascination, her big eyes wide, her hand to her pretty mouth. 'Oh my!' she breathed. 'Oh, how dreadful!' as the lawyer's clerk, inspired by her rapt attention, recounted item after item, mounting the case for staying resolutely at home on terra firma.

When the train stopped at the first station, Allbones had abandoned the terrors of the third-class carriage for the relatively unalarming cattle wagon. Here, the light was dim, strips of light penetrating the gloom from the open vents. Three hundred and fifty assorted ferrets, stoats and weasels in their cages. Three thousand pigeons cooing and flapping behind drawn tarpaulins. Allbones sat on the crate amid their comfortable stink, rocking with the motion of the train. In his coat pocket Pinky dozed comfortably as the past raced away and the future came rushing on.

Somewhere up ahead in the first-class carriages rode Eugenia and her grandfather. The same country flew past their windows, framed by mahogany and tasselled blind, though the rattle of its passing was softened by horsehair and velvet. Allbones had seen her at the other end of the platform as they were preparing to leave. Just a glimpse, but it was enough. She was on the same train, seated by a window, rocking to the same rhythm of iron wheels on iron rails. He imagined her face at the glass, her hands folded on her lap, and that indeed was how she sat.

She is looking out the window, her book open but unattended on her lap, and it is her favourite book, too. *The Natural History of Selborne*, a birthday gift from her grandfather, who prefers her to read reality and not the romances so often preferred by young women. He is reading, but then he has passed this way many times before on his way to the city to attend some lecture on some topic of interest: the discovery of a rare orchid perhaps, or a previously unrecorded creature of surprising habits, the report of the retrieval at great risk of some treasure. Pursuit by tigers or surly savages, unforgiving deserts or inaccessible mountain kingdoms ruled by unpredictable despots. He reads his book while she sits with one finger holding her place in Selborne, looking out the bleary window as the products of natural history race past. And perhaps she thinks too of the young man she glimpsed that morning, loading his crates full of ferrets into the cattle wagon at the other end of the platform. Perhaps she thinks of him seated on the same train, watching the same scene, and of the long grass on a summer afternoon, the pressure of his lips on hers.

Seated among his ferrets, Allbones is imagining fire at sea, or the smash of a ship mid-channel. He is imagining a maiden trapped within the burning ship and how he scrambles over flaming timbers to her rescue. He is not deterred by smoke or fear. He ignores his own peril to climb a fiery stair, to find her cabin, where he lifts her in his arms and carries her near-senseless body to the safety of the lifeboats. Or, better yet, he swims with her on his shoulders — he swims well, lithe and sleek as an otter — until they are both rescued, and as the great ship sinks beneath the waves he carries her to some tropic shore where, among giant ferns, her eyes flutter open, she knows that she owes her very life to him, he bends to kiss her tremulous lips . . .

The train with its cargo of young and fearless travellers enters the city. Through the vent, Allbones can see ranks of buildings, houses like the cliff faces where pigeons nest in their hundreds, inhabited here by flocks of people. The chimney-pots are black with smoke from their fires and washing hangs on poles from grubby windows and in the narrow streets he can see shops and cabs and a dense press of humanity all busy and preoccupied, like the creatures you find when you overturn a stone: that buzzing, skittering horde.

The first glimpse of water is between a forest, a winter forest of bare trunks, being the masts and spars of barques and sloops and clippers, with a scattering of the sturdier stumps of steamer funnels. All drawn up at their loading berths where their bowsprits form a parallel guard along the length of the breastwork, each bearing its sign: the *Sea King* for Shanghai. The *Yorkshire Rose* for Capetown. The *St. Ives* for Trinidad and Valparaiso. All settling beneath their due loading of Birmingham steel and Manchester cotton and Staffordshire china and engine parts and furnaces and knives and guns and patent medicines and all the production of a million busy mills and foundries.

And here is the ship, the one Allbones and his ferrets will travel on: sixth from the gates on the right. For Wellington direct. This splendid clipper, the *Adam and Eve,* 999 tons, (reg.) 100 A1 at Lloyds, under the command of Captain Scruby, to sail as above on October 1. For freight or passage, apply Shaw Savill and Co.

He stands at her rail watching the commotion below: the cranes swinging their heavy burdens from dock to hold, guided by the shouts of sweating men, the wagons drawing up to discharge, then trundling empty away through the iron gates that keep the press of emigrants from boarding until the ship is made ready for them. The milling crowd cluster at the iron gates talking to those who will stay behind, uneasily aware that the words they use should be weightier than the words for normal conversations and that they should be saying something memorable, but in the bustle and strangeness, with the ships waiting and among a crowd of strangers, the conversation is stilted and stiff, constantly interrupted by wagoners shouting "Way! Look out there!' so that they have constantly to part, to move aside so that they see beyond the passing wagon their own family grown strange and distant already. For the first time the emigrants see their fathers as old men, bowed down through decades of deference, they see their brothers as clumsy and old-fashioned in their buttoned coats, their sisters as timid creatures, out of place among this crowd of adventurers. And the emigrants feel already a twinge of impatience at their determination to remain here, staying home in their warm burrows where nothing can ever change. The emigrants can see their ship and the glimpse of water beyond, where tugboats and lighters bustle. They can see the frail threads that hold the big ships to land, threads that in only a few hours will be unknotted to release them into the great experiment.

Allbones stands above, watching them all in their best going-abroad coats and hats as if they were dressed for church. He sees the child running through the gates as if it cannot wait for the newness to start. He sees the young man eager to leave his clinging sweetheart with promises of future reunion once he's there, once he's got things settled, when she can come out to join him. He sees the cluster of young girls, country girls with pink cheeks and unfashionable skirts who still wear their hair plaited, unlike the city girls whose hair is knotted on top, then hangs loose about the shoulders.

The country girls are noticing too: they plan to emulate the style the minute they get on board and have a berth and time to devote to themselves.

They mill about waiting for five o'clock when the carpenters will have finished. An army of men is at work on deck and between decks, sawing timber, hammering, drilling, whistling and cursing, working as fast they are able to transform this solid cargo ship into a vessel capable of transporting 412 humans and their assorted necessities, not to mention 202 ferrets, 66 stoats, 82 weasels and 3200 pigeons. Allowing one pigeon per ferret per week, given a voyage of average length at around ninety days, the ferrets will dine regularly on fresh meat, supplemented by whatever wildlife can be found on board: mice, rats, stray seabirds . . . They will dine like kings.

Tethered by the lifeboat that will serve as a manger, six goats bleat dolefully, and a pen has been constructed behind the galley to house a Dorset bull. Four Tamworth pigs — three sows and a boar — are penned behind the cookhouse, and alongside the pigeon cages stand half a dozen crates containing a raucous rooster and several dozen hens to keep the emigrants in fresh eggs. Straw for the animal emigrants' bedding is stacked in the hold, along with baled hay and sacks of wheat and barley for their feeding. Coal is heaped there too, to cook the human emigrants' food, and a consignment of iron rails to carry them on the new railways that will be constructed over primeval rivers and untamed ravines. And windowglass that will frame their new view. And wines and spirits in hermetically sealed barrels to toast their safe arrival. And crates of nails and tools to build new homes and candles to light them and china to lay on new tables and ball bearings and clamps and a consignment of fob watches to set the proper time and four pianos and a harmonium.

By mid-afternoon some order was beginning to emerge from the morning's chaos. The 'tween decks had been subdivided into compartments: one at the rear for the single women, a centre saloon for families and married couples, and a compartment in the foc's'le for the single men. Narrow berths had been knocked up running fore and aft, two deep and eighteen inches wide, for the reception of their consignment of statute adults as calculated long since by the exporters of slaves and convicts. Bare timber stood ready for the emigrants' mattresses. Pegs awaited their coats and bonnets. A table awaited their mugs and plates and a lamp hung so that they would be able to continue with their reading and sewing below decks should the weather prove inclement. Barrels held fresh water. All was order and calm. The rich lanolin smell of the wool that had occupied the hold for several months faded into the resin of newly sawn timber. Allbones stood at the rail sniffing lanolin and timber, the fatty reek of humanity emanating from the narrow alleyways of the city, and the dank stink of the river and the faint salty whiff of the sea, which lay in wait only a few miles downstream.

The ferret cages formed a solid wall in front of the raised poop deck and the first-class cabins that stood beneath it. Hammered firmly into place to withstand the strongest blast, the cages occupied the area between privilege and expediency. On the one side, rosewood veneer and velvet piled carpets, dining saloon, spacious cabin and the poop for promenading. On the other side, on the main deck, tarred timber and the hatches that led down to steerage. At either end of the ferret cages were two large cages filled with pigeons, whose flapping and woodland cooing was soft among the screeching of gulls.

Allbones had come aboard early with Fowler to supervise the installation of their stock, watching anxiously as the crates were carried aboard, then nailed into place by a couple of ships' carpenters who clearly found these country lads a joke. Serpents and anchors coiled about their forearms.

'You be careful with them creatures,' said Fowler as they shoved a crate into its place on the framing with a firm kick. 'Them's worth four shillin's a head and a bonus for every one we gets there hale.'

'Hale, eh?' said one of the carpenters, cocking an eye at his mate. 'Four shillin's a head! Well, fuck me!' He booted another crate in as his mate smirked. Fowler's face flushed, his bogie eyes took in two directions at once and before either carpenter could react he had them both by the throat and their heads were knocked smartly together, as if he were cracking coconuts won at a fair. Trapped in a murderous headlock, pressed hard up against their own handiwork, the carpenters resisted, using techniques perfected in a thousand quayside brawls. They twisted and fought to turn hammer and drill on the big man, but he was too strong for them. He had them in his fists and would have broken them, had a voice not interrupted from overhead. A peremptory voice, accustomed to instant obedience, a voice that cut through the shouting and cursing as easily as it issued orders in a raging storm with a massive sea running and a howling gale tearing at sail and rigging. It ordered Fowler to stop, to cut it, or he'd be off the ship. Fowler hung on blindly in that dumb mastiff way of his.

'Drop 'em!' said Allbones. 'You heard what he said!' And

Fowler saw reason at last. He was not about to be thrown off the ship before the journey had begun. A phantom flickered in his dull brain, a dusky maiden unbuttoning her skirt. He released his grip.

'There'll be no fightin' on this ship,' said the stern man in the smart cap. 'Any more of that, and you're put ashore. Understand?' Fowler understood. The carpenters stood beyond his reach, rubbing their skulls. 'And there's to be no trouble in future either,' said the man in the cap. 'You're a big lad, but one step out of line, one wrong move from you, and we drop you over the side. That clear?' Yes, said Fowler. That was clear. He straightened his cuffs, set his hat straight, and the carpenters went back to their work, but a little more respectfully, now that the value of the cargo had been pointed out to them.

'That's more like it, lads,' said Fowler. There was to be no threat to his investment. He had added his own store of ferrets to the total before they left Ledney, including at the very last a white hob he called Sultan.

'That's my hob,' said Allbones, knowing it immediately from the kink in its tail and the broken claw on the right forepaw. 'That's Pompey!'

'Izzat right?' said Fowler, uninterested. 'Well, blow me!'

He was happy: good money in his pocket and on his way to the islands. 'He's not a bad hob. Not the best I ever had, but not bad.' And he offered to split for him: two shillin's. He could afford to be generous.

Pompey peered through the netting, pink nose riffling as the welter of new scents assailed him from all sides. Smoke and timber and river water and the thrilling stink of females on heat. At least a dozen awaited his services in cages to his left, his right, from above and below. He scrabbled at the wire, seeking a way through to their receptive haunches.

Allbones had his berth too, his eighteen inches against a wall of temporary planking, smooth to the touch and still smelling of its return cargo of wool and flax and kauri gum. Fowler had taken the upper berth immediately beneath the hatch so that he could, as he put it, lie at his ease and see the stars as they sailed through the warm seas toward the dusky maidens. Allbones would not see much of the stars down there on the lower berth. He could not even sit upright. He stored his bag in the six inches provided beneath his berth and felt a flood of longing for an empty road on a summer afternoon, the wide wood on a moonlit evening.

The feeling of confinement intensified at six o'clock when all the emigrants were finally permitted to board and the single men's cabin filled with forty others setting out their mattresses and bedding. Through the partition separating them from the married quarters a deafening racket of children squabbling and a woman complaining that there simply wasn't room, there wasn't room for so many, and a man was arguing with another that with four children they should have the berth at the rear as it was slightly larger and the one who had taken it had no children at all, and someone was hammering up a shelf and there was the racket of several hundred bags and boxes being unpacked and their contents being put in their proper places, clothes hung on the right pegs, plates and cooking pots and knives to the racks beneath the table, and all this conducted in a babel of English with accents from Scotland to Devon and Welsh and Irish from the Kerry hills, and the tongues of Uist and Mull and Whalsay and Orkney, along with four Germans from Hanover and a couple of young Swedes, all off to dig gold or cut timber or clean houses, to make a living somehow in the new country. And beyond the noise of the main saloon was the chatter and laughter of the young women settling into their cramped quarters, two to a bed, in the stern, and from overhead the bark of orders and the thump of the sailors' bare feet as they moved about, preparing the *Adam and Eve* for her departure.

And at last, as the moon rose, swollen orange through the smoky air of the city, they rocked away from the dock, drawn out into the basin by a tug puffing mightily with the importance of the moment. And the emigrants waved into the darkness at the shadowy figures who had remained until the last moment, a handkerchief flickering from the dock like a moth's wing.

'Goodbye!' the voices called. The cries of migratory birds. 'Goodbye!'

Allbones and Fowler were already at work. There was water to be poured from the barrel into each tiny bowl, and the remains of a butchered cattlebeast to be cut into portions for each animal. The pigeons had to receive their ration of Bartholomew's Patent Bird Food and a sprinkling of grit, followed by a tasty savoury of hemp seed to celebrate the commencement of the voyage.

'That's me done,' said Fowler, stretching. A dozen cages remained to be serviced but Allbones could see to it, while he sauntered off to join the press of passengers at the rails for a last view of London. Left alone, Allbones worked on, fighting his way through the crowd, for all four hundred and twelve crammed the main deck on this moonlit night, delaying as long as possible the moment when they must retire below to lie restless among so many for their first night aboard. They stood about, delighting in the unseasonably warm night air, which seemed like a good omen, and the slight rocking of the ship, which was not half as bad as they had feared. From their pens the goats bleated and the bull stretched his heavy neck and lowed piteously, but the passengers were soothed by the balmy air, which already seemed to carry a whiff of the blue Pacific on its breath.

Allbones tried to ignore their presence but it was difficult. He had never been trapped among so many people before, not even on fair day or in the market at Brinkton. He felt a bubble of panic in his throat and a fierce urge to ask for release. There were small boats darting about them as they made their way downriver. He could still take his bag and ask to be set ashore, he could resign from his position forthwith and leave Fowler to continue if he wished. He had no desire to see this island with its naked girls and omnivorous rabbits. He could go home, walk back down the lane to the Bottom End where Mary Anne would welcome him and the littl'uns would surround him, eager for news of his great adventure, going to the city on the train.

But even as he imagined it, he knew it was unlikely. The city already seemed far off. The ship's rail marked the boundaries of existence. And there were creatures here that needed his attention. They were small and, while fierce enough in their own territory, here they were defenceless. They needed him to feed them, and water them, and fetch them clean straw and keep them well. He had lifted them from their appointed place among hedgerows and fields and woods, where they were safe and could lead the lives they were intended for. He had purchased others, buying them from breeders the length and breadth of the country who had tended them, each after their own fashion, all their lives.

And now it was his task to convey them, whole and sound, to the other side of the world. Fowler would never manage it on his own. He could handle a dozen, perhaps, or twenty. But three hundred and fifty? And thousands of pigeons? Impossible. The big man leaned complacently against the rail, smoking his pipe and eyeing the bevy of young women who had been allowed up, this once, onto the deck after nightfall, to see the country pass, under the close eye of their matron: a former governess who had made this journey twice before for the Female Emigrants' Society and delivered all her charges untainted and morally uncorrupted. She was not to be easily fooled. The girls milled about, chattering and giggling and pointing out the sights.

Allbones ignored the claustrophobic crush and concentrated all his attention on the job in hand: feeding, watering. And eventually he was done. Ferret, stoat and weasel burrowed down into their dry straw, contented with their lot, and Allbones was able to find a space between the ranks of cages where the straw was stacked in bales and covered in tarpaulin and he could sit unobserved and unjostled, out of sight of the crowd. He sat on straw that smelled of a hot afternoon, cuckoos calling, a dragonfly darting overhead, and peered out at the full moon setting its billowing sail above the jagged skyline of warehouses, stores and tenements.

She had not boarded with the mass of emigrants. She came aboard at Gravesend two days later among the other cabin passengers. He could see her fair hair blowing in the stiff breeze that was making all the smaller boats on the river bob and tip. She clambered aboard awkwardly, clutching a small cage and holdall, and disappeared through the door between the ranks of ferret cages that led to the first-class cabins beneath the poop deck.

Allbones was dusting the pigeon cages at the time, checking for mites. He saw her pass only a few feet away and, at the sight of her, he felt all his doubts subside: she was there and close enough at all times to touch, though he was below decks and she was above.

The ship edged out into the Channel, past the mudflats of the river estuary and the reefs and glimmering towns on a coast as foreign to Allbones as any distant isle. The sails gathered a hesitant wind and the ship took on a slight lean, inching away from England, and the world began to shrink: to just this vessel, two hundred and eighty-eight feet of iron frame planked with teak, her hull sheathed in shining yellow metal, her main mast soaring over two hundred feet above the deck, her spars bearing three and a half acres of sail.

To just this crowd of men and women and boisterous children, just this captain with his shrewd eyes and full whiskers, just these sailors, barefoot and ruffian, sprinting up masts as if they were trusty oaks with their roots set in steady soil, clinging to the spars preparing for the 'Go about!', when the whole world swung over to a new angle.

The work was simple and repetitive. At first light, Allbones crept from his berth to fetch Fowler his mug of hot tea from the cookhouse on deck, where a massive mulatto kept charge before the stove with its leaping flames and retinue of restless pots and swaying kettles. A cup of tea first thing. Not too strong. With two spoonfuls of sugar. When Allbones had suggested he go and get it himself, Fowler had scowled. He reminded him who was the assistant here, and who the head keeper. And, as always, it was simpler to comply.

Allbones liked the early time anyway, from the first day when the sun rose in a blur of crimson on ships waiting to be drawn upriver, emerging from the morning mist like the ghostly castles in some children's story, and on ships like their own heading out with a fresh crew. He liked the relative quiet, broken only by the bark of orders from the bridge, before the passengers woke and arrived on deck with their noise and talk. He liked being part of the quiet, purposeful world, before Fowler emerged, blinking and dishevelled an hour or more later, to help with feeding the stock.

Pitford had come to inspect them soon after he embarked at Gravesend. He stood splay-legged before the ranks of cages, pleased with their appearance of order and well-being. This shipment at least would succeed: no taint of the shipping fever that had so far plagued every consignment of livestock, whether cattle, sheep or ferret. On this voyage, no animal of his would collapse with grotesquely swollen head, gargling for air as the fever took its toll. This transportation would be a model enterprise. Solid housing, a varied and appropriate diet, a wooden ship that would not overheat in the tropics nor judder as steamships were reputed to do. Every detail had been attended to. These creatures would be transported as comfortably as could possibly be arranged. And, most of all, they would be in the care of expert handlers.

'There will be a bonus, remember!' he had said, clapping Allbones and Metcalfe on the shoulder. 'For every creature brought safely to port! Good luck, lads!' As if they were both off to battle.

Allbones glimpsed Eugenia sometimes among the other cabin passengers, walking about on the poop deck a few feet above his head. But she made no move to speak to him, nor to wave or indicate that she had seen him there at work before the rows of cages.

Slowly, slowly England slipped away, until it was the smudge on one horizon while the smudge on the other was France. Out into the Bay of Biscay, where the currents converged and the ocean began to play in earnest with sails and keel and human invention. It tossed the *Adam and Eve* into the air, then caught her deep, groaning and growling through the hull, rattling chains and stays and setting the sails to moaning. The ship was beaten like a hollow drum. And the passengers lay, brought equal in the ocean's heavy paw, prone on steerage bunk or on fine linen in the first-class cabins, vomiting the same clear bile when their stomachs had emptied, vomiting into whatever receptacle they could find, whether hookpot or china basin, or simply vomiting where they lay, for there was little point in niceties when they were all doomed to die by drowning.

They vomited and prayed, the Irish rattling away at their Ave Marias, the English reciting their Our Fathers, the Germans and Swedes praying after their fashion, while the sailors' feet thudded overhead day and night, though day and night were an interchangeable grey blur.

Fowler moaned face down on his mattress, his pudgy hands gripping the sides of the berth. Allbones could see his fingers from where he lay below on the lower berth, the knuckles white with the effort of holding on, lest he be thrown out entirely onto the floor, where vomit slopped with seawater leaking through the rim of the hatch cover overhead. Allbones lay on his back, watching the boards of Fowler's berth buckling under his weight as he was rolled magisterially first this way then that by the great waves. So much for the stars. So much for the dusky maidens. On every side in the darkness the other lads moaned too, and retched and muttered their prayers. The stench was overpowering — of vomit and urine, for the closet was on deck, on the far side of the closed hatch across a bleak and bucking, wave-dashed wilderness, and only a madman would attempt the journey. They voided where they lay, like cattle in a wagon.

Allbones could bear it no longer. With difficulty he extricated himself from his cramped berth and staggered, knocking elbows, fighting for balance on the bucking craft, up the companionway.

'Where you goin', you daft bugger?' said Fowler, between retches.

'Got to see to the ferrets,' said Allbones, lifting the hatch cover awkwardly. Cold air rushed in, laden with spume.

'Oh,' said Fowler, with absolutely no interest. 'Them.' His investment could starve for all he cared. It was probably going to drown anyway, along with every creature on board. They was all goin' down . . .

The deck was a slippery slope and the horizon swung about as the *Adam and Eve*'s sails were buffeted by a Biscay gale. All the livestock were stowed beneath tarpaulins that had been securely lashed down. Allbones struggled to keep his feet as he fumbled at a knot and lifted the canvas. Underneath, the air was as thick as a fenland fog. Rich, delicious, familiar. Allbones breathed it in luxuriously.

The fact was, he was not prone to seasickness. Not in the least. His body simply rose and fell with each rolling swell and left him unperturbed. For a man who had spent his entire life on land he was as easy as any sailor on this ship as she heeled over, full sail set, for her captain, Scruby, was a racing man with a hundred pounds riding on seventy-five days, port to port. Boyd had managed seventy-six and a half to Dunedin, Sutherland eighty-two to Auckland. The *Adam and Eve* was heavy laden but by God, she could fly when she was driven with a strong hand. The crew had their bets on too, so hard over, she leapt away while in steerage and first-class cabins her cargo heaved and moaned. Only one had ventured forth. Alone on deck, Walter Allbones fed titbits to his ferrets and refilled water containers emptied of their contents on one tack or the next. The pigeons huddled in their cages with their heads buried beneath their wings, unless tumbled from their perches, when they flapped about the floor in consternation at this suddenly unsteady universe.

The door to the first-class cabins stood closed at the centre of the ranks of cages. Only a few feet away she lay, perhaps pale and listless, her brow damp with sweat, her hair touselled on the pillow. Allbones severed the wing from a pigeon carcass and snapped it at the joint. Her long hair, tangled and unbrushed . . .

The door suddenly opened, caught in a gust of wind. There she was. Hanging on to the jamb as the ship lurched then righted itself. She steadied herself and forced the door shut, then turned to face into the wind. It tore at her hair and she clutched the lapels of her coat before it could be stripped from her shoulders. She found her balance and glanced about.

'Mr Metcalfe!' she said. 'Isn't this thrilling?' The deck lurched. Her eyes shone, her cheeks were flushed with a warm colour he had never seen back when they were safe on solid earth.

154

'Don' know about thrillin',' said Allbones. 'It's a mite jumpy in my opinion.'

'So why aren't you lying below groaning like everybody else?' she said.

'Got to tend the ferrets,' he said. 'Besides, I don't fancy drownin' inside a box. I'd rather take my chances up here where I can see what's what.'

'Tosh,' said Eugenia. 'We shan't drown. Though everyone, absolutely everyone, is saying we shall. Even my grandfather is frightened. I've never seen him so low. I'm going to fetch him some hot coffee, to settle his stomach.'

From the cookhouse they could hear the cook standing by the boiler singing nonchalantly of Nancy and her charms. Tags of song blew from the open door between lulls in the boom of wind and wave.

Allbones stood at the chopping board with the bloody blade of the Ledney knife open in one hand and a dismembered pigeon in the other, a fitful sun breaking cover to dapple the deck, and felt a sudden burst of joy. To be here with Eugenia in the midst of the ocean where everything was being tossed about, flung into the air and who knew where it all might fall! Eugenia bent down to peer into one of the cages.

'How are they?' she said. 'Are they seasick too?'

'They're quiet,' he said. 'But a ferret's a ferret. They must eat every day.'

Eugenia set the coffee pot she was carrying on the chopping board. 'I'll help you if you like,' she said. 'My grandfather won't mind. He won't even notice I'm gone. Here . . .'

She held out her white hand.

'You sure?' said Allbones. 'It's mucky work and they stink.'

Other passengers had already complained, objecting that they had not known they were to share their vessel with vermin. But Eugenia shrugged it off.

'I've already told you: I've no sense of smell. And the other keeper I presume must be sick, so . . .' She picked up some gobbets of bloody meat and began dropping them into the cages. The ferrets smelt blood. They left their nests and snapped at her fingers, tearing the meat with their tiny white needle teeth.

The ship rose and fell and the crew clung to the spars above like a flock of black rooks to bare branches on a stormy day and Eugenia stood with Allbones talking about the other cabin passengers: the bumptious little ex-tailor who had gone to New Zealand, found gold and returned Home to show off his good fortune and also to find a wife; a poor meek milksop who clung to his every word and said 'Yes, Mr Tonks.' 'No, Mr Tonks' as if his every utterance were God handing down the tablets of the law. And the tiresome family of children — six of them with their parents and a governess in the stern cabin, where they shouted and squealed day and night and were generally insufferable, though the father read them lengthy prayers every morning to which no one seemed to be paying any attention, while his wife remonstrated with them ineffectually and told them to be little ladies and gentlemen: they bounced and kicked and tumbled about, and Eugenia had seen the father fondling the governess in the corridor when he thought no one was observing. There was the doctor who was to act as ship's surgeon for the duration of the voyage. Kindly enough if a little vague, and no use whatsoever as he, too, had been struck down by seasickness and was as incapable as his charges of leaving his berth. And the two prim ladies on their

156

way to the colonies to take care of their bachelor brother but in reality, no doubt, to find husbands for themselves, for clearly they had had no luck in Cheltenham. Not that that should cause any surprise, for the older sister was pinched and irritable and the younger cared only for her dog, a bad-tempered terrier called Tray who yapped incessantly, especially when Eugenia's nightingales sang. She had brought two, a pair, which she hoped to release in New Zealand, for she simply could not imagine a country devoid of the nightingale's song, no matter how charming the songs of its native species.

'I know that, scientifically, birdsong is nothing more than an expression of territorial possessiveness or an attempt to attract a mate,' she said, 'but I cannot resist the conviction that the call of the nightingale is much to be preferred to any dreary piano sonata.' She clasped her hands earnestly.

Allbones shrugged. 'Don' know about the pianner,' he said, 'but a nightingale's song is pretty, no doubt about that.'

Suddenly the ship was crammed with incident. Released by the storm, Eugenia chattered and Allbones listened, loving her mimicry of the pompous little tailor, the mincing wife, the grandiloquent doctor . . . The passengers kept to their berths, the crew went about their tasks. No one paid any attention to them both, as they worked their way along the cages, stopping from time to time to hold fast to the framing when wave or wind took the ship by surprise.

'I'm glad you're here,' she said when they had finished and she was wiping her hands clean on a cloth. 'I had not been well, but truly I have felt one hundred times better since we came aboard . . . And now, I suppose I should fetch my grand-father his coffee . . .' The ship lurched mightily as she said it and she staggered so that Allbones had to catch her to prevent her from falling. From the circle of his arms she laughed up at him, the two of them delighting in the playfulness of the sea, the unexpectedness of touching.

'I'll hold you steady to the cookhouse,' said Allbones, and he placed his arm about her waist. They set off like two dancers joining a set, jigging a few steps this way, a few steps back, across the slippery deck to where the cook was singing that he'd pay Paddy Doyle for his boots while calmly stirring a boil-up of beef and potato for the crew's dinner as if it were the most natural thing in the world to cook at an angle of forty-five degrees, reaching uphill for the spoons and downhill for the pepper.

'So,' he said as they stumbled into the dark galley, laughing at their tottering progress, 'there's a couple of true sailors among the lot of yez after all!' The whites of his eyes shone in the dark and his black skin gleamed like coal in the glow of flame from the stove. His accent was strange to them both: a melodious singsong that rose from the depths of his broad chest, and there was laughter in it too. He filled Eugenia's coffee pot, then poured them each a coffee in a tin mug, for they might as well have a drink now they had nego-tiated the deck, so they stood there, comfortably sheltered from the wind and the rain while he told them about America, where he had been born, where there were swamps and alliga-tors that could take a man in a single bite and how he'd run from there to take ship and circle the world, from Africa to the snow and ice, and he'd done this run so many times he'd lost count and she was a good ship, the *Adam and Eve*, and Scruby a fair captain and they'd nothing to fear . . . The ship heaved and went about to commands that were tossed by the wind and the cook held the steamer steady with a practised hand and it was warm in the cookhouse and they were safe, and true sailors.

Then they slid and lurched back over the deck once more, Allbones holding Eugenia close so that nothing spilled from the coffee pot, and at the door to the cabins she turned and kissed him, a quick light kiss on one cheek to thank him for his assistance. Then she was gone.

Allbones tied down the tarpaulin, feeling the press of her lips on his skin and the press of her body warm through his coat. When the tarpaulin was trim, he went to retrieve his blanket from below decks. As soon as he opened the hatch cover the stink of sick men billowed up and in the dim light he made out Fowler's huge recumbent body, prone on his berth.

'Do you want anythin'?' he asked, for he could be generous now, to a sick man. But Fowler merely moaned and rolled on his side, so Allbones closed the cover on them all and found a place to sleep, in the straw behind the pigeon cages. It was dry there under cover, and he dug into its prickly, familiar shelter and buried himself in the warmth of a summer afternoon with cocksfoot and trefoil and clover. Insects crawled about, for they also liked it for their bed. And through the wall behind his head Allbones could hear the murmur of voices. They were muffled, but one of them, he was certain, was Eugenia's.

The next day she returned, late in the afternoon, on the same pretext, coffee pot in hand. And the next. And the next. As the *Adam and Eve* ploughed the waters of the Bay of Biscay she and Allbones stood shoulder to shoulder in the half light of the sheltering tarpaulin, feeding ferrets and talking. She told him about India where she had been born: a hot country, as far from the grey walls of the north Atlantic as it was possible to imagine. The sun baked the red earth until it cracked open and everything was brilliantly coloured and there were the most astonishing birds and animals everywhere: elephants, for example, and tigers. (Her father had shot fifty tigers!) And crocodiles that lived out the dry season in deep burrows like badgers only much, much bigger than any badger: huge creatures, with jaws that could kill a cow. They lay in their burrow, not eating or drinking for months, until the rains came, when they went back to their swamps. Swaying beside him on the deck she talked about it with longing: Poona, Bombay, Rawalpindi. The names sounded rich and exotic. She and her mother had gone with her father sometimes on his expeditions, because her mother, though frail, loved to be in the high mountains where the snow lay permanently. They were carried on chairs by porters up narrow paths between banks of flowers, heaps of them everywhere and most of them unrecorded. That was where she had learned to draw, seated with her mother sketching plants while her father went off with his shiakree, shooting. He had collected a great many specimens and even had a bird named after him: the Himalayan snow finch, *Montifringilla Pitfordii*. Unfortunately he did not live to learn this: both her parents had died. First her mother, of cholera, then a few days later her father. She had been sent home to England, to the care of her guardian, her grandfather . . .

In return Allbones told her about Ledney — the Ledney he knew, which existed beyond the walls of the big house. At first he was hesitant. There was nothing interesting about him, or the village, it was just ordinary. But she asked questions, who and what and when, with the same kind of attention she paid to insects or the habits of birds, and he found himself telling her about the littl'uns, and Mary Anne going into service when she was ten like all the other girls of the village, and how the boys stayed on to work in the fields or at the bankin, and the way he went out with his ferrets, after rabbits.

'So that's what you were doing the night we met?' she said, poking a wing through the netting so that the ferret inside played tug o' war with her.

'Yes,' he said. He could tell her the truth. He could tell her anything at all.

'I envied you,' she said. 'So free and easy out there on your own. At ease among the trees and knowing your way about.'

The life he described to her was as exotic, as strange as India. They talked until she sighed and said she must fetch the coffee or her grandfather might miss her and wonder where she had gone and then, arm in arm, they did their own odd, uneven dance back and forth across the deck, from the cook-house to the cabin door.

Then the kiss. Each time, the kiss.

7.

It has been universally remarked that all new
colonies settled in healthy countries, where
room and food were abundant, have constantly
made a rapid progress in population. Many of
the colonies from ancient Greece, in the course
of one or two centuries, appear to have rivalled,
and even surpassed, their mother cities.
Syracuse and Agrigentum in Sicily, Tarentum
and Locri in Italy, Ephesus and Miletus in
Lesser Asia, were, by all accounts, at least
equal to any of the cities of ancient Greece. All
these colonies had established themselves in
countries inhabited by savage and barbarous
nations which easily gave place to the new
settlers, who had of course plenty of good land.
It is calculated that the Israelites, though they
increased very slowly while they were
wandering in the land of Canaan, on settling

*in the fertile district of Egypt, doubled their
numbers every fifteen years during the whole
period of their stay. But not to dwell on remote
instances, the European settlement in America
bears ample testimony to the truth of a remark
that has never I believe been doubted. Plenty of
rich land to be had for little or nothing is so
powerful a cause of population as generally to
overcome all obstacles.*

Malthus, *Essay on the Principle of Population*,
Vol. 2, Everyman's Library, 1958 p. 304

The storm abated. The wind fell and the sea, having proved its
point, no longer wished to play. It calmed to a rolling swell
through which the *Adam and Eve* charged south before a brisk
and steady wind. The cloud broke and a tentative sun left a
thin rim of pallid light about the rim of the hatch covers.

Down in the dark the emigrants stirred, feeling the ship
steady. They rolled over in their tangled bedding. They sat up,
and felt about for their combs and collars. They were not
drowned after all. They were still alive. Their fervent prayers
had been answered. Or perhaps there had been no risk after all.
They felt a little embarrassed, perhaps, at their cries and terror.

The hatch covers were lifted and fresh air poured over
them, smelling of the wide open sea and the great adventure
they had planned back by the hearth at home. Daylight
showed their pale faces, their tangled hair, their dishevelled
clothing, stained with the evidence of their previous and now
faintly ludicrous panic. They straightened their hair, rinsed
face and hands, made themselves presentable and, blinking,
climbed from their noisome burrows into sociability on deck.

They queued at the cookhouse with their pots and plates for their dinner. They sauntered to the rail and looked out calmly at the ocean. They observed the captain at the helm and the practised agility of the crew. 'He's a good man, that Scruby,' they said to one another. They were in good hands: God, the captain, the crew. And the *Adam and Eve* was a fine ship.

Fowler, too, rose from his sticky berth and lumbered up in the shirt and trousers he had pressed beneath his mattress to a tidy crease. Delicately, so as not to dirty his attire, he helped Allbones roll back the tarpaulins. In their cages the ferrets were dazzled by the sudden bright light. They screwed up their pink eyes and licked their fur as they awaited their daily rations. The water was already taking on a dank taint and they turned up their noses at the leftovers from the emigrants' table: no salt beef and plum duff for them. The goats ate the scraps, just as they accepted the wood shavings left by the carpenters or some ancient newspaper treasured since London as a last link with home but now rumpled, stained and illegible. They chewed with equal dispatch on month-old parliamentary debate and brutal murders in Whitechapel, reports of massacres in distant climes and fashionable dress for the cooler season. The ferrets drank the dank water and accepted bread and condensed milk as slops on the understanding that every third day they would be rewarded for their forbearance with raw meat, bleeding, just as they liked it. Then they squeaked with pleasure and gnawed the pigeon bones clean.

Allbones and Fowler chopped and tended, though their minds were not fully on their work. Fowler had made a quick survey of the single women aboard and had selected as his particular quarry a pretty young milliner from Woking, with dark eyes and curling black hair. And Allbones watched for Eugenia.

Now the sea had calmed, she no longer came to talk to him by the ferret cages. Pitford had found his sea legs and walked about the poop with the other cabin passengers, making his observations. He trailed a line from the stern in search of strange fish. He dissected and skinned a mollymawk, taking it with a single shot as it hovered over the ship so that it fell neatly onto the deck at his feet. He netted a nut he spotted drifting upon the surface of the ocean and identified it as the fruit of the cocoa tree, *Theobroma cacao*. He gave a brief lecture on its nature and cultivation to the cabin passengers, showing them the brown seeds nestled within the white membrane from which that familiar beverage, hot chocolate, was manufactured. He sat reading on deck beneath the sail which, when the days grew warmer, was rigged over part of the poop to provide shelter from the tropical sun. Another sail stretched over the main deck, beneath which the emigrants could recline at their leisure, to sew or read or play desultory games of cards.

Rush-splash rush-splash went the ship's hull, surging through the Atlantic. *Whick-whack whick-whack* went her billowing sails and *yappy-tak, yappy-tak* went her stays, and there was the rattle of chains and the thud of the sailors' feet and the squeal of children, the crying of babies, the chatter and talk of four hundred and twelve statute adults.

Allbones saw her sometimes, seated on a stool while her grandfather sat reading on his deckchair with the brim of a white straw hat shading his broad brow. She usually had her sketchpad open on her knee, recording the small events of the day: a shark taken over the rail lying on the deck waiting for her grandfather's scalpel. A steamer passing them to starboard bow, trailing its plume of smoke. An Irishman seated on a barrel playing the fiddle for dancing. The nights became warm, stiflingly warm, and the passengers delayed returning below deck for as long as possible. They danced jigs and reels beneath a full tropical moon before exhaustion finally drove them back below to fetid air and restless dozing. The single men abandoned their berths entirely and dragged their mattresses up and slept in the open, lying looking up at the stars swinging overhead, a little way this, a little way that. The single women were less fortunate, being herded by their brisk matron to their quarters soon after darkness fell and firmly locked away from temptation until daybreak.

Eugenia may have been only inches away, but among the constant press of people there was never an opportunity for conversation. The poop deck was as remote as some glass mountain, and she was the princess at its peak, beyond his reach.

In this strange warm season the ferrets became confused. Like the pigeons, which had begun to moult in the sudden heat, they presumed these warm days to be spring come round again unexpectedly and that winter must have passed them by without their noticing. They went into heat. The cages were filled with hobs with testicles swollen to pink marbles and sluts languid with longing. The stink of musk filled the air so that the passengers complained of the stench, and kept their distance as far as that was possible. Passing the cages on their way to the cookhouse they held their noses and averted their gaze. Allbones and Fowler worked their way steadily from cage to cage, supplying each female with an enthusiastic hob. The squealing and shrieking of coupled animals penetrated even the usual racket of the ship. It caught at the edge of hearing, a painful pitch that set the teeth on edge. Dozens of ferrets to be carried hob to slut, left for the two hours it took to complete coition, then removed before the slut wearied. Every second day, until the swelling subsided and the two keepers knew the ferrets were safely serviced and in kindle. By the time they got to Wellington their investment would have quadrupled, or more. Tiny, naked and blind, but worth their weight in hard cash. That's if they could get them there without mishap. That's if the sluts were able to feed their young. That's if the kits did not succumb to fleas or colds or bloat.

Allbones dropped Pompey in with a receptive slut and watched as the hob grasped her neck and shook her savagely. The slut squealed, tail up and haunches quivering. Pompey could on occasion become carried away, biting until the sluts bled, and once he'd torn the head completely away so that Allbones had returned to find him still mounting a lifeless corpse. He was strong and sired fine kits, but he was not to be trusted. But this time he seemed to be settling to his task without undue savagery and the slut seemed unafraid. Allbones closed the cage and moved on down the line.

Through the railings above he could see her. She was dressed in white and wore a broad-brimmed hat tied on with a blue scarf so that it would not fly away in the little breeze that was dancing over the wide ocean to play pitpat with mainsail and top gallant. Even from this distance he could detect the smell of soap and clean linen and a hint of violets, among the denser stinks of melted tar and hot timber, salt beef boiling in the galley, sweating skin and that pungent odour of cockroaches, which in the tropical heat bred by their millions in every cranny of the boat. Beside her, her grandfather sat on his deckchair with one finger holding his place in his book, though his head was tipped back and his mouth had fallen slightly open and he was dozing. She glanced up quickly from her drawing, pencil in hand, and across the crowded deck she smiled, the briefest of smiles. The sweetest of smiles. Her hand lifted in a discreet wave.

His heart rose. He whistled as he opened another cage and inspected its resident. They had to be careful not to overwork the hobs for there were few of them and they could not rest while there was mating to be done. They scratched the walls of their cages, desperate for coition, though their fur might be matted, their eyes dull from lack of food. They could, if not properly cared for, die of lust. The deck shimmered in the noonday heat.

When he went below, it was to be greeted by howls of protest. 'Jesus, but you're a stink, the pair of yez,' said one of the Irishmen, slapping down a king and nothing else to occupy him until they came ashore in Wellington.

'Can't be helped,' said Allbones. 'They're all come in season and if they're not mated they'll die.'

'Sure and I understand them completely,' said the Irishman. 'That's myself, so.' He leaned to one side and released a pungent fart. Who was he to complain about the stink of ferrets? They were all bloated on salt beef, plum duff and stale water. The single men's quarters was a noisome place of furiously competing odours. He slapped a cracked navvy's hand on the table. 'Full house!'

Allbones was resigned to stinking. Fowler, however, was discontented. He tried to hang his clothing from the end of the berth to air it. He helped himself liberally to a bottle of scented Macassar oil belonging to one of the Germans and smeared it on his bald skull as if he were polishing the knob on a banister. He washed his face and hands morning and evening, using soap and more than his fair share of the water. The other men were able to dive over the side when the ship lay becalmed of an evening, once the women were safely below deck. But Fowler could not swim, deterred as a boy by his watchful ma, who told him tales of fairies with mushroom skin who lay in wait just below the surface of river or dyke channel, ready to drag down the unwary child. He waited mournfully on deck as the others splashed and dived in the still, deep waters of the open ocean.

Allbones was more fortunate. He raised his arms and flipped from the rail, hitting the water below with scarcely a ripple. The water closed over his head and, with his eyes open, he swam alongside the glinting yellow metal sheathing of the hull, then rose into the night air, his arms and legs coated in gleaming phosphorescence that ran from his body in streams of light. He lay on his back as the others dared one another to swim under the ship all the way to the other side. Go on! Go on! He lay and floated, looking up at the vast hemisphere of stars overhead. This was not like the river at home, flowing between leafy banks of Queen Anne's lace and bowed willow with a base of soft, sucking mud. This was one vast world of air and stars and water, limitless, beyond imagining . . . Something brushed against his leg and for a second he was clutched with fear: something had risen from the darkness, something sinister, unknown. It could wrap its tentacles about him and draw him down, down . . .

It was just the rope, of course. The rope ladder that hung over the side by which he could climb back to the deck. He grabbed it and scrambled back to where Fowler waited, steaming and stinking.

Fowler had attempted several times to engage the pretty milliner. It was not easy, for the matron was experienced and knew all the tricks: she had them off to bed at seven on the dot and maintained a careful vigil during the long tropical days, keeping them busy with little tasks: sewing shirts, using fabric and thread thoughtfully provided for just this diversionary purpose by the Female Emigrants' Society.

It took cunning to circumvent her. Fowler tried dawdling at the cookhouse when the emigrants were milling about to collect their dinner. But she was always with other girls, one of a giggling circle, and never seemed to notice him. Black curling hair, lustrous brown eyes . . . He stood by the door, as the mess's portion of beef cooled, waiting to catch her eye. He returned irritable, slamming down a dish of meat in a slimy coating of congealed liquid.

'You're bloody lucky I goes for it at all!' he said.

He was not accustomed to frustration. What he wanted, he took. But this girl — her name was Lizzie, that much he had been able to elicit from one of the gigglers — eluded him, peeping from beneath her fringe of curls, hiding in the midst of her starling flock. He began to fancy himself, for the first time, in love. He moaned for her on the long warm nights, pressing his great bulk into the prickly mattress.

'Lizzie,' he moaned against the ticking. 'Ah. Lizzie . . .'

'Lizzie, darlin' Lizzie!' mocked the Irishman and his mates, but carefully. Once Fowler had woken mid-dream and heard them laughing. He had snapped wide awake and fallen straight to rage, dragging one of the Paddies by the neck around the cabin, hookpots and plates set to tumbling in all directions, the lantern smashed so that the candle within fell and set a tiny flame licking at someone's bedding and he'd

have had the whole ship alight and them all in the lifeboats
rowing to God knew where had someone not upended a jar of
pickled onions over it while others dragged Fowler from his
prey. Now, though the Paddies laughed when they saw the
great bulk of the man yearning, they kept it discreet.

Allbones watched him look over his shoulder from
tending the ferrets as the girls emerged each morning and
spread about the deck to brush and braid one another's hair.
The girl was not to his taste. She was undeniably, as Fowler
said, the prettiest of the bunch, but there was a calculating
glint to those dark eyes that hinted at trouble for whoever fell
in love with her. He did not envy Fowler's longing. For he, too,
dreamed when he lay on his berth, hearing the muffled sound
of the couple through the temporary planking that divided the
single men's quarters from the family cabin. The wood was
thin and there were gaps through which, when he woke from
a dream of dragonflies and long summer grass, came a whispering so close it might have been in his own ear. He listened
to this couple. He thought he knew them: a sturdy farm
labourer from Lincolnshire and his fretful wife, four children
already tucked to sleep on the top berth and another swelling
visibly beneath her skirts. At night, as the ship lazed down
through the tropical latitudes, he heard them whispering
among the snore and whiffle of sleeping passengers. The
furtive creak of bed timbers, the rhythmic beat accelerating
amid all the other thuds and creaking of a ship sailing through
the dark. The muffled groan of the man forcing his mouth into
the pillow, the swiftly suppressed sigh of the woman. Allbones
slid from his berth then and took blanket and pillow to the
straw behind the pigeon cages. He lay there beneath the
swaying constellations, dreaming of whoever he wished, out of

sight of this little world's mockery.

Fowler finally had his chance on the night they crossed the line. There was a line, the captain told them, that ran about the earth, like the belt around the plump belly of the globe. When they crossed this line it was customary for every ship to celebrate. There were games in the afternoon: a king wielding a trident, the cook transformed to his demon wife, rough treatment with tar for the novices and dunkings in a trough rigged from a sail on the main deck. And rum afterwards and dancing by the light of the tropical moon to fiddle and banjo and a couple of accordions. In the mêlée, as all the dancers changed partners in a wide circle, Fowler saw his opportunity. The little milliner danced toward him, twirling from one man's hand to another all the way down the line and finally she was his. He took her hands in his. He stepped sideways one two. He said at last the words he had been practising.

'I think you're the prettiest girl on the ship, an' I've bin wantin' to talk to you for weeks.' There was no point in holding back. She turned under his arm and at last he held her in his arms for the spin.

She looked up at him with her dark eyes and said, 'Ta. But — 'scuse me mentioning it — what's that funny smell?'

Ferrets. Bloody ferrets.

Fowler watched her spin away from him to the next man, one of the Irishmen who, though straight from some western bog and speaking scarcely a word of English, could dance like an angel. Light and lithe on his feet, he swept the girl up into a flying jig that had her breathless and laughing and clinging to his waist as if her life depended upon it. He spun her and held her steady and she was able to match him. Her little boots tapped the planking in a rapid tattoo and then they were off, her skirts swinging wide, her dark curls bouncing with such perfect balance that all the other passengers stood aside. They let them have the floor and watched instead, applauding their skill and grace. Fowler did not wait to watch. He abandoned the set completely and slouched off below, where Allbones found him an hour later, scrubbing hard at his hands with a bar of marine soap.

'Once I leaves this boat,' said Fowler grimly, 'I never wants to see another fuckin' ferret as long as I live!' The cabin smelled of lye and sweat and dirty mattresses. And still, without any question, of ferrets.

Allbones left him to scrub and sulk and joined the others on the deck. Eugenia stood among the first-class passengers who did not care to join the emigrants in their boisterous dancing, but who had been drawn nevertheless by the Irish fiddlers and the whoops and laughter. They lined the poop deck rail to observe the hilarity on the main deck below. Allbones leaned against the bulwarks with a couple of other reluctant dancers among the single men, tot of rum in a metal cup. He could see her clearly, tapping her hand in time to the dance. Her grandfather stood close by her shoulder, with an expression of pained amusement at the goings on before him.

She was looking well these days. Pink-cheeked, no longer the pale wraith he had seen at the window. She was listening to something one of the cabin passengers was saying, her head inclined slightly. As she listened, her eyes were on the dancers, who were forming sets for the Lancers, four by four and eight by eight. He could see her frowning slightly and the way her eyes moved restlessly from one group to another. Then, suddenly, she saw him. She saw his face looking up at her from among the crush of hundreds of people. She smiled. A sudden,

173

open, delighted smile. Her hand lifted in a barely perceptible wave. She had picked him out and once she knew where he was standing, her gaze returned again and again. She had picked him out. He was the man she was looking for.

From that night on, he lay on his bed of straw looking up at this new southern sky. The stars were shifting, taking on new patterns he had never seen before. Through the wall separating him from the first-class cabins he could hear the movement and muttering of others. Pitford, perhaps. And Eugenia sleeping on white linen.

Down through the latitudes they moved. Tacking to west and then to the east until the cook said they were past the Cape of Good Hope. 'And now won't Scruby have her flyin'! Hang on to your hats, me boys!'

The ship headed south. Scruby drove her down, down, down through the latitudes to where the wind blew strongest and the curvature of the globe on its way to an icy nothing lessened the distance to be covered before landfall. The clouds, which the passengers had almost forgotten existed as they dawdled through the tropics, gathered once more overhead and they looked out warmer clothes from their trunks: shawls and coats and gloves and scarves. Clothing they had stored away for weeks past during the sunny idyll. Beneath their feet they felt the ship begin to buck, scenting the wind. Her sails filled and the deck became a slippery slope to be negotiated with care. In their cages the pigeons, bare of feather from their unseasonable moult, shivered. Their naked wings offered no protection from the sudden cold. They huddled among their own droppings, unable to fly up to their perches. They trembled and flapped uselessly. Their eyes glazed and the ferrets fed well, and Allbones worried that after this glut they might run out of fresh meat long before the voyage ended.

Fowler chopped up a carcass and said he didn't care much, one way or t'other. The ferrets wouldn't object to eating one another, once they were hungry enough. He was bitter with rejection, glowering and fierce, and the motion of the ship was making him queasy once more. His fingers were frozen.

Where was this sunny isle with the dusky maiden slipping from her skirts to stand invitingly before a forest of ferns? A gust of hail splattered like grapeshot on his bare skin. Beneath the hatch, Lizzie sat with her friends, chatting or whatever it was they did down there in the half light now the days were cold. Whenever she saw him now she looked away swiftly as one of the starling girls nudged her and said something to make her colour. It was not reassuring. He stank, he felt shrivelled, cold to the marrow and sick, and he didn't care if not a single ferret survived to land on this frozen wasteland to which they seemed, after all, to be directed.

His knife slipped and nicked his thumb. 'To hell with this,' he said. The pain took a second or two to register as blood oozed from frozen skin. He flung the knife down. 'To hell with it all!' He sucked the wound and, lurching on the icy deck, crawled off to sulk on his berth.

Left alone, Allbones attended to his charges. The ferrets felt the cold too. They huddled down in their straw. He had given them a deep litter, but even so, many of the cages were now empty. Their occupants had sickened in the tropical heat, lain limp in his hand without even the urge to nip his fingers. Bellies quickening with young, they had gurgled as they fought for breath. Then their necks swelled and they died. A dozen a week sometimes, though he tried sulphur and every remedy at his disposal. They were dropped over the side, like

175

the children who took the measles in the cramped quarters
below deck. Measles and a kind of pneumonia not unlike the
disease that was carrying off the ferrets: lethargy, fever,
coughing, asphyxiation. A quick death. The children were
carried in their parents' arms to the rail, where the captain read
a brief service, then they slid over the side as simply as if they
were sliding from beneath their mothers' skirts. Their bodies
made a tiny distant splash and by the time the ship had sailed
another minute, there was not a ripple left behind.

Nearly a hundred animals had died, despite Allbones'
care: seventy-three sluts and twenty-one hobs. Thirty-three
pounds in bonuses! A year's income for a bankin-man back
home in Ledney. As the *Adam and Eve* heeled over hard into a
wind with ice and snow on its cruel breath, Allbones put all
his effort into conservation. He had the mulatto cook add
warm water to their slops, and plumped up their straw
bedding. He kept the tarpaulin drawn to protect them from
the great waves that gathered about the ship, taller than
houses, taller than cliffs, before slamming across the deck,
sweeping its full length so that men grabbed frantically for
whatever was to hand to stay upright. One of the crew was
caught in the open before the wheel and swept over into the
terror of tempest and oblivion but was carried back by a
following surge and deposited in the rigging.

The Dorset bull was less fortunate. It was swept away
along with its pen, which splintered beneath the force of a
wave as if it had been made of paper. Allbones watched it go
from his place by the pigeon cages, keeping a firm hold as the
water foamed about his legs, grabbing at his ankles. The bull
moaned as it went. He could see its head raised above the
water and its legs swimming frantically up the steep green

slopes of the sea as if it were running across some buttercup hillside, then the crest broke over it and it was gone.

Whenever Allbones looked up, it was to see the crew clinging to the spars like rooks on a storm-tossed pine, laying out every inch they dared, for each man had his bet on their arrival. They were sailing with Scruby and in hope of the record. Their bare toes curled like claws around the thin security offered by a bucking wire. At night as he lay tucked down in the straw behind the pigeon cages under the tarpaulin he could hear the thud of their feet and the bark of orders caught by the howling wind.

Let go the fore bowline and haul taut the weather braces!

And still they headed south. As the weather worsened, the decks emptied of all but the most intrepid passengers. Stowed below decks like all good cargo, the emigrants dozed on their berths in the dim light shed by a candle lantern, or chatted desultorily as they picked at their clothing for lice, those grey armies that had marched up every seam and occupied every crevice. Here, a woman kept herself occupied by knitting, plain and purl, plain and purl, across the endless ocean. There, a man whittled a tiny sailing ship with flags flying. They played endless games of rummy. They argued, gossiped, avoided those whose presence had become intolerable but who had to be endured for who knew how many more weeks. They told the children to behave or they'd get a belting, or played the fiddle until someone told them to shut it, they'd had enough of 'The Maid of Mourne Shore' to last them a lifetime. They prayed when a heavy sea hit them, but without their former desperation. A dull resignation had taken over. In the lazaret a woman gave birth to a healthy boy, while another groaned and cried out for twenty hours, then gave birth to a dead one. The emigrants sat, feet braced at a steep angle, or slept pressed downhill against one another, until the go about, when they rolled in the other direction.

From time to time, necessity drove them on deck. Allbones met them sometimes when he emerged from beneath the tarpaulin to fetch fresh water or to dispose of a small dead body. He could not quite bring himself to feed his ferrets to one another, though he knew they would be indifferent to cannibalising their own kind, in fact would welcome the fresh titbit. But it seemed indecent. He tossed them into the sea instead, where they flipped about on the gale or were seized by some seabird. A gulp, and they were gone. The passengers staggered drunkenly up the icy mountain to collect the midday meal: more salt beef, more roly poly, more hot tea. The return, hands laden, was even more problematic. Timing was all: a lull in the wind, a break in the ranks of waves and off they tottered, sloshing tea and fighting to hold the beef in the pot. The hatch cover lifted. The passenger disappeared. The cover closed.

Allbones sat in his snug nest, boots braced against the pigeon cages, and chewed on a biscuit between tasks.

And one afternoon, just as it was getting dark, the edge of the tarpaulin lifted.

'Hello,' she said. And she slid in beside him. 'My grand-father's poorly again and everyone else is playing charades in the cuddy. I loathe charades. They all choose such boring words and I can't act at all. I said I had a headache.'

The cold suited her. Down here where the land had turned to solid ice and floated on the horizon, she had a high fresh colour. Her cheeks were pink, her hair a glossy fall. She was plump under her thick woollen coat. She had a little fur collar and a white fur hat.

'That's ferret,' he said. 'Your hat's made of ferret skins!'

She laughed. 'If your ferrets are as warmly clad, they will be happy!'

'They're confused,' said Allbones. 'Don' know if they's Arthur or Martha or what season it is. Your hat's a winter pelt. These creatures is all fitted out for summer. There's dozens dead. And the pigeons moulted weeks back so they're poorly too.'

'My nightingales too,' she said. 'They used to fly about my cabin, but now all they do is sit in their cage and mope. And they have stopped singing entirely . . .'

As she said it, the ship was hit from starboard and she was flung at him by the force of the sea that walked over the deck, its long white fingers feeling into every cranny, smashing at the tarpaulin and threatening to drag them all away. Icy water sucked at their legs up to the waist, soaking through to the skin. They held to the framing of the cages and to each other as it fingered their bodies, considering. He had his arm about her, she was pressed close against him, the fur of her hat tickled his chin. Slowly, tortuously, grinding mightily, the ship righted itself. The water drew back. But off the bow another wave advanced, its crest white like snow on a high hill.

'Quick!' he said. 'In here!' The straw behind the pigeon cage still had a core that was relatively warm and dry. He showed her how to burrow down, until they were lying close amongst dry stalks of grass, still bearing the scent of a distant summer. He dragged the blanket over. They lay face to face, soaked and shivering, both bodies trembling with the shock of the icy water. Body to body, face to face. Her breath warm on his chilled skin. His arms pulling her close. They drew warmth from each other. Through her coat he could feel the curves of her. She felt less wraithelike now after months at sea, more real somehow: plump beneath her thick winter clothing and firm where some feminine business of laces and whalebone formed a tight corseting carapace. But her cheek against his was soft and smooth. He could hear the surviving pigeons cooing in the cages behind him, their call a soft counterpoint to the howl of a southerly gale as it had once accompanied a summer afternoon amid leafy woods and the whirr of dragon-flies. He shivered and felt her shiver too. But now it was not the cold alone that made them tremble, but the closeness, the strangeness of coming close to that moment when you step ashore onto the new land that is another's body.

His hands ran the length of her back, her hands felt their way beneath his coat, finding the greater warmth near the skin. Down here under the tarpaulin, the light was dim. They felt their way about like creatures newborn whose eyes were yet shut. They moved slowly, pausing at each new place as if it were a plateau where they could linger, kiss.

She was a landscape of skin and hair, scented with soap. He was a region of bone and muscle, flat where she was curved, hard where she was soft. They stroked and touched through bulky winter clothing, tenderly, without haste. Something held him back at the point where Lardy Annie would have dragged up her skirts and said, 'Well, come on then, let's get it over with!' and Sally would have waited, placid as a cow in a field, for him to be done so that she could return to her blackberrying.

And at last she said she must leave before she was missed

and she stood quietly as he picked straw from her hair and her coat, preparing her for the dash back to the cabin door. He watched her go, heard the shout of laughter from the cuddy as the door opened, smelt the whiff of cigar smoke. Then the door closed and she was gone.

But she returned the next night. And the next. Allbones drifted through the days, working automatically from cage to cage, mucking out, mixing slops, filling waterbowls from the barrel where the water was red, three months since it was poured from a spigot in Camberwell. It stank and sported a rainbow skin and the passengers complained of the strange taste to their tea. The ferrets had no option but to drink it, snatching what they could before it spilt as the ship took another battering. Their straw was musty, though Allbones changed it often. The wood of their cages sprouted tiny white toadstools. They fed well nevertheless, for one of the goats had died, choking on a splinter of wood gnawed in terminal boredom from the side of its pen, and the Tamworth boar also waned. Its flanks shrank until every rib was visible, before it rolled on one side and sighed its last, its pale eyes closing on the inner vision of an endless oak forest scattered with acorns and belly-deep in the soft sweet balm of muddy earth. Its meat was rank and salty when butchered, too salty for the passengers to stomach, so the ferrets feasted.

Fifty-one days out from Gravesend. The *Adam and Eve* was charging for the record, leaping across successive lines of longitude at an average speed of eleven and a half knots.

When Allbones did venture below, Fowler was there, losing at poker and in a foul temper. He looked up from another worthless hand as Allbones scrambled down, releasing a blast of chill air into the fetid warmth below.

'Shut that fuckin' hatch,' he said. When the waves came over they leaked through the hatch cover directly onto his berth below, so that his bedding was permanently sodden and his clothes impossible to dry. He would have taken Allbones' berth instead, but there was not enough headroom. He could not even sit up down there without hitting his forehead. So he put up with the damp, as they all had to. So much for lying looking up at the stars. Through the thin partitions dividing cabin from cabin he could sometimes hear girlish laughter from the stern where Lizzie and the other girls were safely stowed. It drove him to distraction.

One of the Paddies was dealing. He looked up as Allbones fumbled among his belongings for the trousers he had spread to dry as much as was possible under his mattress. The ones he had on were sodden. His socks, the ones Mary Anne had knitted for him so carefully before he left, were rotting, and his new boots were ruined, the leather cracked right through by repeated immersion in seawater.

'Now, why would you be stayin' out there,' said the Paddy, 'freezin' yer balls so?'

'Because he's a mad bastard, that's why,' said Fowler. Four of clubs. Three of diamonds. Nothing of any use. Again.

'Got a girl up there?' said one of the Welsh miners.

'A sweet little dolly to keep him warm,' said another. 'Double.' He slapped a half-crown down.

Allbones flushed despite himself. 'Someone's got to look to the ferrets,' he said. 'They's worth good money.'

'Someone's lookin' to your little ferret an' all,' said a Londoner. 'Cookie tells me you been makin' yourself nice and comfy under that tarpaulin.'

Fowler turned to watch him narrowly.

'Izzat true?' he said.

'No,' said Allbones. 'Course it's not true. It's a howlin' gale out there or hadn' you noticed?'

The men were bored. They were tired of cards, tired of one another's company, tired of being stuck in this cabin with some bugger's feet in your face and some other bugger farting.

'Why're you getting' all dandyfied then?' said the Welshman, making a grab for Allbones' dry trousers before he had a chance to drag them on. 'I think Archie here might be right. I think you might have a dolly out there. Don' you think so, Mick?' He balled up the trousers and tossed them to a mate on the other side of the cabin.

'Don' be daft,' said Allbones, hopping about bare-legged. But it was too late. They were ready for a game, something to pass the time. He was a diversion, with his skinny white legs. The trousers flew about. Fowler grabbed him by the arm.

'Is he right?' he said.

'No, he's not right!' said Allbones, squirming in that familiar powerful grip.

'Oh yes I am,' said Archie. 'Cookie told me. Says you been goin' at it like a pair of rabbits.'

'Kissin' and fondlin',' said another.

'Oh, darlin' Lizzie!' said one of the Paddies. 'Oh, darlin' Lizzie, won't I love you for ever!'

Fowler's face darkened.

'Izzat her name?' he said. 'Lizzie?' His grip tightened.

'Oh, Lizzie, Lizzie!' sighed one of the men, flinging himself dramatically into the lap of another in a parody of passion. 'Kiss me, Lizzie!'

'Shove off,' said the one chosen for his attentions, and

tipped him onto the floor so that the man landed hard and the mood slid suddenly in the direction of anger.

'He's just makin' it up!' said Allbones frantically. He kicked, landing a blow on someone's head or chest. It landed with a dull crack. 'I'm not seein' any Lizzie. I don' see anyone. I just does my work. There's a lot to do on my own with you down here all the time.'

Fowler slammed him hard against a berth end so that Allbones could hear the distinct crack of something, a rib perhaps. Around them the cabin had erupted into a scrum of flailing arms and legs, while the tall Scot, who wore glasses and took the readings on Sunday and was headed he hoped for the ministry, stood up on the table saying, 'Gentlemen! Gentlemen! Please! Control yourselves.'

A tin cup whistled past his head and despite his grave demeanour he was quick enough on his feet. He ducked and the cup landed fair and square on Fowler's skull. For a second Fowler's grip weakened as he turned to confront this new assailant, this lanky misery who had preached at them ever since Gravesend and made a great thing of kneeling by his berth before retiring each night, hands clasped in sotto voce prayer. Moreover, he spent his Sundays tucked up in the main cabin with a little study group who included a pretty young blonde, the eldest daughter of a sturdy baker intent on bettering himself and his family's prospects in the promised land. She gazed up at the Scotsman adoringly from beneath a pert little bonnet as he quoted long and lovingly from Paul's Epistle to the Ephesians or some such sweet talk.

'You're irritatin' me,' said Fowler, bogie eyes swivelling. 'You know that, MacGregor?' He reached over, though the Scot was saying it wasn't him, it wasn't him, all dignity and thought of brotherly forbearance cast aside, and Allbones was able to take advantage of the distraction. He gave a mighty wriggle, found by a miracle that his trousers were to hand, landed by accident onto his own berth. Scrambling and dodging he dragged them on and was able somehow to get through the mêlée of grunting, punching bodies to emerge into clear air.

'Hello,' she said later, after a murky day had turned to night. She slipped in with him under the tarpaulin. Their little tent, their tiny shelter in this tempestuous world.

They lay side by side looking up through a gap in the tarpaulin at a rare patch of clear sky. A half moon rode like a ship across rags of cloud, and though the air was bitingly cold they were snug in their straw nest beneath a shared blanket. She had brought a bottle of brandy with her.

'My grandfather has had his draught,' she said. 'He won't miss it.'

The brandy left a warm star in the belly, spreading out to toes and fingers. They took turns at it. 'Look,' she said, pointing up through the gap over their heads. 'The Southern Cross.' The stars hung four square in the place where the Pole Star used to be. Whole constellations had shifted while they had been travelling. They had moved aside, sunk out of sight, tipped upside down, swung to new configurations.

'It's all different, isn' it?' he said. 'I didn' know it'd be so different.'

'It's because of the earth's axis,' she said. 'Some constellations are . . .'

'I din' just mean the stars,' he said. 'You . . . me . . . we're different. . .'

185

Allbones smelled him before he saw him. A rich aroma, part fruitcake, part pork. There was a flicker of candlelight in the gap over their heads, then the gap in the tarpaulin widened as it was drawn aside and a bulky shadow intruded between them and the constellations of the southern sky.

'So,' said Fowler Metcalfe, peering down at them from the roof of the pigeon cages. 'This is where you gets to. You sneaking little bastard.'

He dropped down heavily beside them as they scrambled to their feet. 'An' who's this slut yer got with yer?' Eugenia had her face lowered, but he forced her chin up so that the light from the lantern fell full upon her. He peered at her closely.

'Oh,' he said, momentarily taken aback. 'Oh, it's you, Miss.'

'Yes,' said Eugenia, making an effort to recover her dignity. 'We were observing the stars.'

At that Fowler started to laugh. 'Izzat right?' he said. 'Yer. An' I'm the man in the moon.' The narrow gap behind the pigeon cages was tight with their three bodies. He held up the lantern and looked around, taking in the pile of straw, the tangled blanket.

'My!' he said. 'So Cookie was right! Isn' this snug? So this is what yer been up to all these weeks. My, my, my. The lip of a strange woman drops as an honeycomb and her mouth is smoother 'n oil. Who'd a thought it, eh?'

Allbones took Eugenia's hand. He could feel it tremble. He placed himself as best he could to shield her from Fowler and what he knew, if they were already up to biblical quotations, must be coming. But Fowler was in no hurry. He leaned back against the cage wall, enjoying the scene.

'So, how long has this been goin' on? Since we came aboard? Or longer, mebbe? Mebbe this is why you decided to come along after all? When I was thinkin' it was the offer of money, or the sea air. Good for the lungs, innit? Clears the chest. But I were wrong, weren' I? You was just after a bit of skirt.'

'Don' talk like that in front of Miss Pitford,' said Allbones.

'Oh,' said Fowler, smiling dangerously. 'Beggin' your pardon, Miss Pitford.'

He made the name an insult. A flame came to life behind Allbones' eyes, a scarlet glare too bright to see the other man clearly by. His silly face, his shiny skull, his fat red libidinous lips. Allbones' arms rehearsed a blow to those lips, the splitting of skin, the trickle of blood . . . His other hand was in his coat pocket, clenched by sheer reflex about the reassuring haft of the Ledney knife. He felt the flame flicker and build until Fowler was a blur. Fowler might have been aware of it but he was unperturbed. He gazed instead up at the southern sky and considered his options. He had a proposition to make.

'What's it worth, eh?' he said. 'For me to keep mum? Not to tell a certain party what this young lady has been up to while her grandfather lay sick in his berth?'

'You're disgusting,' said Eugenia. 'Vile and disgusting.'

'I think someone round here might be disgustin,' said Fowler calmly. 'But I don' think other people'd think it was me that was disgustin'. Not a certain party who does not like to be upset. Not in this pertickler instance.'

Allbones squeezed Eugenia's hand. 'You'd better go,' he said. 'I'll deal with him.'

Fowler leant over and patted her arm familiarly. 'Don' you

worry, Miss Pitford. Your little secret's safe with me.' His teeth gleamed like a row of white pickets in the candlelight. 'An' if there's any dealin' to be done, it'll be me that's doin' it. This twistin' little bastard is goin' to do ezzackly what I say.'

Which was that Allbones was to continue to attend to the animals and hand over all his pay to him, Fowler Metcalfe, without comment or objection, along with all bonuses, when they received their packets on arrival in New Zealand.

'An' in return, I'll say nothin' about what I've seen here this evenin'. I wouldn' want to blacken this young lady's reputation. Even though in my opinion she's no better than she ought to be. Just a slut like the rest of them.'

That was the point when Allbones lunged. It was also the point when Eugenia kicked out. She was small, but surprisingly fierce when cornered.

She hissed and spat and kicked the big man hard on the leg with one of her little pointed boots. Fowler had not been expecting attack from that quarter, not from someone in a fur tippet and hat. And in the split second it took for him to register surprise, Allbones also struck and the Ledney knife with its broad blade made one fast, fierce cut to Fowler's hand, cutting through flesh, severing tendon and artery to the bone. A two-edged sword.

Fowler howls.

He drops the lantern.

The lantern falls.

Its light traces an arc in the darkness.

The glass shatters and the candle touches straw: the dry nest Allbones had found at the centre of the stack. A stalk of dry fescue. Then another. There's a crackling as the candle flame locates the sunlight trapped within each blade of grass. A leap of light. The fire runs along some stems and finds the wall of the pigeon cages, coated against the elements in creosote and tar. It pauses, but for no longer than it takes to lick, taste and find the wood to its liking. The fire is hungry now and dancing around them all and they are stamping, beating at it with bare hands. Within the cages the pigeons have woken and are flapping the featherless stumps of naked wings in panic. From up on the rigging the crew have looked down and seen it too. The flare of flame by the poop deck. The nightmare: fire on a wooden ship. Their craft burned to the waterline so that only the iron frame remains. The blackened remains drifting, sinking, the lifeboats bobbing with their survivors on the wide empty acres of the Antarctic Ocean. The slow demise to cold, to hunger, to thirst. Skin peeling to bone. No record of their passing. They disappear . . .

'Get out! Get out!' cries Allbones to Eugenia as the flames burrow into the straw. He pushes her through the gap between the cages and wriggles after. Fowler cannot follow them. He is too big to squeeze through, though he howls and pushes. Then somehow he gathers the strength to scramble up onto the roof of the pigeon cages, emerging from beneath the tarpaulin like some character in a play: the Demon King rising from the stage hatch, blackened and fearful.

The bell is ringing the alarm and the crew are racing to form a chain, passing buckets hand to hand. The commotion has woken the passengers in the first-class cabins and, equal now before the force of fire as they have been already made equal in the face of wind and water, the passengers below deck waken also. Doors and hatches are flung wide and the people tumble forth, fighting arms into coats, struggling for a foothold on the slippery slope of the deck, clutching in their arms children who think this pandemonium is not real but part of their usual restless dreaming, just a nightmare from which they will awake in the morning.

They join forces with the crew, all shouting, though the words are largely indistinct, just the bellowing of frightened stock, their eyes white and rolling with terror as they fight to douse the flames, while in their cages the ferrets squeal, escaping to the farthest corners, trapped by timber and netting.

And this time, danger is averted. Water wins. The flames sizzle and die. Burnt straw. Grey ash. Charred wood. Singed feathers. The passengers stand by as the crew check methodically for any sign of rekindling. They huddle in small groups, weeping, soot-stained, breathless with relief. For though death by water had seemed a fearsome fate, death by fire seemed worse. They stand, arms about one another.

'Let us give thanks!' says the lanky Scot, who only a few minutes before was kissing the baker's daughter, on the assumption that this might be all the time they would be spared together on earth before eternal union in heaven. But here they are, safe and sound. He presses his palms together in prayer. 'We give thanks, O Lord,' intones the future minister of the parish of St Andrew's, Palmerston North, 'for this our deliverance in time of peril . . .'

In the silence that has fallen upon the ship, the groaning becomes audible. A deep groan. A woman's voice.

'Oooh . . . ! Ooooh . . . !'

Eugenia is bent over in the midst of the crowd, her arms wrapped tightly about her body. Her eyes are closed and the sound emerges in long, deep gasps. A woman standing near puts her arm about her shoulders. 'You feelin' poorly, Miss? Don' be afeared. It's all over. The fire's out and we're safe, God be thanked.'

Eugenia quietens momentarily, then another paroxysm takes her and she falls to her knees, grasping the woman's skirt tightly in her fist.

'Oooh,' she moans. 'Oooh . . .'

She is bowed over, gasping for air. The doctor forces his way through the crowd and kneels beside her. The woman strokes her back with broad, calloused hands well accustomed to soothing sick creatures — pigs, cows, people — and stays beside her as Eugenia is escorted below deck to the lazaret where, some hours later, while the whole ship listens, she gives birth to a boy.

Its thin cry penetrates every cranny. A high-pitched wail which, for just a second, Allbones, attending his charges in their stinking cages, mistakes for a seabird. The ship surges on, heeled over on a steady swell, gathering speed after its temporary fright, the record still well within reach. The night sky is paling toward dawn. There is a streak of gilded cloud at the horizon. The passengers look at one another as the baby cries for its mother. But she has turned on one side and refuses to look at this creature that has slid so alarmingly from between her legs. She lies and faces the timber wall, tracing faces in the knots as blood seeps from her, and her breasts, released from months of tight corseting, ache and ooze. The woman who has assisted the doctor on other such occasions — five births now since Gravesend: two stillborn, the others without complication, thank God — holds Eugenia's son in her arms.

'Oh, but he's a bonny wee man,' she croons. Soothed by her

touch, he ceases his crying and, swaddled in a blanket, looks about at this strange world with his clear newborn eyes. 'And he wants his mammy's beastings. Ah, take a look, m'dear. He's come from the Lord knows where, but he's right bonny.'

Eugenia shrugs her aside. She is seeping: tears and blood soak into sheet and shift. Her long hair lies tangled on a damp pillow.

In first class and steerage, the passengers looked at one another and muttered. Pitford had disappeared into his cabin at the first sign of his granddaughter's discomfort and remained there, door firmly closed, as the crowd on the deck dispersed and went their separate ways.

'So,' whispered husband to wife once they had found the scant privacy of their own berth. 'So, what do you make of this?'

'Poor wee thing,' said the midwife to the doctor. 'She were brave, too, scarcely made a sound though he's big: eight and a half pounds I'd be guessing, and there's nothing to her. Not much more than a child herself.'

'It makes me so angry,' said one of the prim sisters seated in the saloon, taking up her crochet for it steadied the nerves wonderfully after one had suffered such shock. 'That innocent girl, her reputation sullied. While some lad gets off scot-free!'

'Perhaps the scandal will be of less significance,' said the other, finding her customary calm in the intricacies of an embroidered tray cloth, 'in a place where society must inevitably be cruder than we are accustomed to.'

'But even in New Zealand concealment will be out of the question,' said another woman, a pin nipped between her teeth as she turned a hem. 'Such a shame. After her grandfather has brought her so far and gone to such trouble to preserve her name.'

They sewed or worked their crochet, fingers flicking the thread in and out, in and out, developing the complicated lacy figure.

'If he is indeed her grandfather,' said the embroiderer, stabbing the needle into a French knot. There. It had been said. The pattern was becoming more complex, an intertwining of many threads.

'Whatever do you mean?' said a small, sweet woman on her way to join her sister who sold fancygoods in a shop in a little village called Otahuhu.

No one troubled to explain. But they paused in their work, looked up at one another.

'Oh, my dear!' they said. 'Oh no! Oh! How shocking!'

For anyone might be anyone here. From now on, anyone might be whoever they said they were. There was simply no way of telling for sure. Any story might do. Setting sail on the wide ocean they had not realised that they were casting aside so much: standards, certainty, belief, trust. Some contaminating influence had permeated the ship through the cracks in the timber that formed the lazaret.

8.

Where inaccessible areas exist, as in portions of Otago, I see but one solution, and that is the introduction of the natural enemy . . .

B.P Bayly, Superintending Inspector, 'Report on the Rabbit
Nuisance', *AJHR 1883 H=13,* National Archives

Return showing the CONTRACTS entered into by the STOCK DEPARTMENT since 1 January 1887
Number to be supplied:
1,712 to Rabbit Inspector Invercargill —   *7/6 each*
10,700 to Rabbit Inspector Lawrence —   *7/6 each*
228 to Rabbit Inspector Outram —   *7/6 sluts, 5/- dogs.*
270 to Rabbit Inspector Queenstown   " "   " "
4,300 to Rabbit Inspector Balclutha   " "   " "
4,550 to Rabbit Inspector Kaikoura   " "   " "

21,760

'Report on the Distribution of Mustelids, the "Natural Solution" to the Rabbit Nuisance', 1 January 1888, AJHR, National Archives

The gossip spread, snagging at attention as the ship turned at last toward the north, heading up from the frozen latitudes and still with a chance at the record. The *Adam and Eve* breasted the southern ocean, every available sail set. A bird resembling a thrush landed on the railing one afternoon, and there was a faint pungent scent to the air, mingled with the now-familiar salt tang of the sea. By night, if the moon were through, the passengers could look out from the rail and see, just below the surface of the water, long trails of luminescence lighting the way to land that must lie just beyond the horizon.

Eugenia had moved to her cabin, where she remained listless in her bed, refusing all food, refusing all contact with her child.

'She just lies there, day in, day out,' said the woman attending her, who was kind-hearted and had had seven of her own and knew the despair that could come with lying in, even when the babe was healthy and did not sicken and die within a few days. Some women simply became sad, the way sheep sometimes rejected their lambs and kicked them away. The trick was to be quiet, to bring the child to her at regular inter-vals, to simply wait until the sadness passed. Sometimes it did and the mother thrived and took her child to the breast at last. And sometimes it didn't, and the woman waned and the child became motherless, suckled by another.

'Too young,' the woman said. 'The young ones sometimes take a while to mother on.'

Meanwhile the weather warmed and the captain had given

it as his opinion that they might be only fourteen days from port and would not, after all, be spending Christmas at sea. The passengers began to move about, recovering their former animation. On a still afternoon with the first land they had seen in two months bobbing by to starboard — only a hump of rock like a Christmas pudding with a twiggy tree set on top like a sprig of holly but at least it was solid ground — their trunks were brought up from the hold. They sat about on the deck, taking out clean linen, preparing at last for arrival.

That was the afternoon Pitford chose to make his first appearance since the night of the fire. He emerged from his cabin and stepped forth into the sunlight, his face pale, his coat and trousers immaculately pressed by the steward. He wore gloves of soft kid leather and held a malacca cane to steady himself against the slow rolling motion of the sea. At his throat gleamed a silver cravat pin. The busy chatter on the deck dwindled away to silence.

'Look at 'im,' said one of the women. 'Fathers a bairn on a girl too young to know what's what, then walks about, cock o' the walk.'

'Playin' the gentleman,' said another. 'Old bugger.' Spit arced to the deck in Pitford's wake.

No one saw who threw it. A man's hobnailed boot sailed through the air and landed squarely on Pitford's back as he turned to climb the stairs to the poop deck to join the first-class cabin promenade. It was followed by a tin plate, still containing its contents. Salt beef dribbled from one shoulder of the immaculate coat. A tin mug followed. Another boot. Pitford turned to face his accusers. Behind him, on the higher deck, the cabin passengers, hearing the gathering commotion, crowded to the rail.

Weeks of see-sawing anxiety, weeks of being forced to spend every moment in the company of hundreds of others, weeks of sleeplessness and poor appetite and gathering irritation with the men who snored and the women who argued and the children who clambered over everything and the bugs that swarmed in their bedding spilled over suddenly, at the sight of the immaculate man, into rage. The passengers crowded about the stairs.

'Shame!' shouted some.

'Bastard!' shouted others less refined.

The mob had risen and civilisation was taking a tumble. Courtesy and the due process of justice were laid aside. Given the opportunity, the passengers of the *Adam and Eve*, sixty-eight days out from Gravesend, could tear this evil-doer to pieces or string him up.

Pitford looked frightened, the bravado of the cravat pin failing him in the face of such fury. He half turned at the third step and attempted bluff.

'Pray, what have I done to offend you?' he said.

'Ye've ruined that poor girl,' called one. 'Ye're not fit to call yourself a man!'

'I have done no such thing!' said Pitford. But there was a tremor to the words that was immediately audible to the crowd, and his brow was damp with sweat, his eyes wary.

'So, who's the babe's father, then?' called another.

The crowd surged toward him. Pitford took a step back and stumbled, slipped on the stair. The passengers jeered as he fought to regain his balance.

But suddenly, from one side, a large man was pressing his way forward.

'Stop!' he was calling as his powerful arms forced the

people aside. 'Leave him be! He's not the man you're wantin'!'

Fowler Metcalfe stood by Pitford like a big bull mastiff over some fallen animal when a pack of lesser dogs is baying for blood.

'It's not him who's the father,' he said. He swung around and pointed at Allbones, who stood to one side, a little apart from the crowd, by the ferret cages. 'It's 'im! That bastard there!'

The crowd fell silent. They turned toward Allbones. All those faces. Pitford scrambled to his feet, dusting off his trousers.

'I seen 'em together!' said Fowler. 'Up here every night behind them cages. They been at it ever since England. An' earlier, it seems. That's why he's on board. Not for carin' for them ferrets. He knows next to nothin' about ferrets. He's here on account of her. For the ruin of this man's granddaughter!'

Pitford looked down at Allbones. For a moment there was silence. Allbones could see the chase of emotions cross the other man's face. Puzzlement, fury, relief followed one another in rapid succession. Finally he settled on an expression of hurt and outrage. Poor man. Deceived by his own flesh and blood and by a man in his employ.

And then Fowler was at him, all the pent-up rage of the past months released in one murderous attack. Fists and boots found their targets on ribcage, head and stomach. Allbones went down before the onslaught, curling to protect himself as best he could, as the blows rained down and the crowd gathered overhead, urging his attacker on, or remonstrating with him to stop! Stop it before you kills him! And finally someone intervened. It took six to drag Fowler away from his quarry and force him below deck, where he was soothed and congratulated for his fervour. For who wanted someone like that as a shipmate? Some weasly little fella who'd get a beautiful young girl like that pregnant when she was scarce more than a child herself?

'You did right,' they said, shaking Fowler's massive paw. 'You was harsh, but you was fair.'

Up on deck, Allbones woke in a puddle of his own blood. Something white lay beside his face, which it took him a moment to discern was a tooth. His gums and lips were too swollen for him to tell which tooth, or if it were the only one to be knocked out. The doctor knelt beside him, relieved to have a live one and not another body to be slid over the side. Fourteen they'd lost on this voyage. Not as bad as the measles on the *Carpathian* in '79, but not good either. He took pride in delivering his charges whole and well, and not just on account of the bonus he received for furthering the good reputation of the shipping company.

He made a cursory examination of skull and jaw. Broken nose, but it would mend. Eyes blackened but still in their sockets.

'All right?' he said. Allbones unfurled legs and arms gingerly. Things cracked and hurt and all of him ached and oozed.

'Bearable,' he said, through a wadding of torn skin.

'Then up you get, man,' said the doctor. 'And keep out of everyone's way till we're in port. That's my advice to you.'

He had no time for men like this one, pleasing themselves, exercising no restraint, prey to every carnal whim. A man needed discipline and a proper degree of moral fortitude or else he was no better than the beasts. No glorious piece of work, as the poets would fancifully have it, but a brute, a clever monkey, as the men of science had proven by the steady accumulation of fact.

He watched the young man creep away, doubled up, and felt that choking revulsion that swept over him sometimes when he was confronted by the human body. He thought suddenly of a cat he had seen as a child, with matted fur and half blind, its back paralysed so that it moved with infinite slowness across the lawn outside the dormitory window. Just the cat, a slow winter afternoon, the rain dribbling on the pane. He shivered, drew his coat about him and went to his cabin, where he took a spoonful of ether — not too much or he became too drowsy, not too little or he was not lifted to that soft, warm place where a kind of inward sun spread its soothing rays. The supply was dwindling: only just enough to carry them all safely through to New Zealand, and another jar for the return journey. He held his nose firmly and forced it down, resisting the natural impulse to gag and spit it up. He lay back on his berth, feeling the drug take its customary effect. For an hour he would dream, read and dream. And for another twenty-four hours he could re-enter that kingdom by the simple expedient of taking just one sip of water. The smell hung in the cabin, sweet and suffocating, like sugar burned in a pan.

Behind the pigeon cages, Allbones curled in the straw, dragging the blanket closely about himself and shivering.

When he re-emerged, it was to find that he had become near-invisible. Lads who had stopped by to swap a joke, men who had nodded at him as he stood by the ferret cages preserving what was left of his stock, eking out the pigeons among the survivors, a wing here, a leg there, women who had smiled at him and said, 'My, you do take good care of them nasty creatures!' — all now ignored him. They looked the other way, biting their lips at the awkwardness of acknowledging his very existence. They told their children to keep well clear. They turned their backs and looked instead at the horizon where a strip of cloud lay, broken by something that might have been a mountaintop or perhaps just more cloud.

Allbones walked among them as if his bruised body were transparent. When he entered the single men's cabin it was to be greeted with 'What's that fuckin' stink? Would you say it was rotten meat? Should be dumped over the side, is my opinion. What do you think, lads?' They sniffed the air elaborately until Allbones made his exit and retreated to the relative safety of his burrow in the straw.

The woman came at two bells, when the ship was quiet and the helmsman held them steady off a rocky coast. He heard the rustling of her skirts and the tentative *tap tap tap* at the wood of the pigeon cages. 'Mr Metcalfe?' she said. 'Are you there?' Her worried face peered through the gap in the tarpaulin. 'She wants to see you,' she said. 'I don' know what else to try for she's that poorly. I'm fearful for her. Mebbe seein' you'll bring her round. Can you come?'

Allbones followed her through the cabin door. Rosewood veneer on either wall, soft carpet under cracked boots creaking on tiptoe.

'Here you are, Miss,' she whispered, opening a door. 'Look who's come to visit you.'

She stood aside as Allbones entered. Eugenia lay facing the wall, a small swaddled bundle lying unattended in a cradle by the bed. Her shoulders seemed unbearably frail, the bones of the neck like a bird's skeleton where her hair, loose and uncombed, tumbled on the pillow. Allbones removed his hat, awkward in a room that smelled of milk and baby, clean linen and despair.

'Talk to 'er,' whispered the woman. 'Go on. I shan't be listenin'. I'll make sure you're not disturbed.' She went outside and closed the door.

Allbones approached the bed and looked down at the baby's tiny crumpled face, frowning with the effort of staying alive.

He laid his hand on Eugenia's shoulder. She made no move. 'Don' fret,' he said. 'You're both well. It's not the end of the world.'

She made no move.

'It happens all the time,' he said, trying in his clumsy fashion to find the words that might offer comfort. 'Plenty girls . . . girls in our village . . . they have babies unwed.'

Back from service unexpectedly. Some unfortunate episode involving the son of the house or the lad who delivered the groceries. Waist thickening suspiciously under tight corseting and, in a month or so, there's another baby to be raised as brother or sister to its own mother and no more to be said about it.

'But why didn' you tell me?' he said.

A tiny tremor that might have been a shrug.

'You could've told me,' he said. 'I'd do anythin' for you.'

He took a deep breath, feeling himself step over some barrier as if climbing a high wall.

'I love you, you see,' he said. For the first time he said the words he had never spoken to a single soul. The words had always seemed a joke, something for girls to giggle over, soft talk. But there he was: saying the words and feeling them sit sweet on his tongue like fair-day marmady.

In the silence that followed he could hear the ticking of the clock on her table, a steady rumbling snoring from the cabin next door, the background sounds of the ship now so familiar that they could be ignored: sail flap, water rushing at the hull, the calls of command from the poop overhead. The baby pursed its lips and sucked rapidly, the way ferret kits suckle in sleep, their dreams all sweet and milky. She lay still under his hand and he could not be sure she had heard him.

'I love you,' he said, to taste the words again. 'You can tell me anythin', won' make no difference.'

She was crying. He could feel her shoulders shake, hear the gasps as she wept into her pillow. He stood beside her, touching her for the first time not as a lad but as a man. A man giving comfort. He stood by and waited until the tears were spent, feeling the crying slow, then hiccup to a halt.

She rolled over.

'Your face!' she said, seeing for the first time the bruises, the torn lip, the broken nose.

'I'll mend,' said Allbones. 'Why din' you tell me?'

'I didn't know,' she said. 'Or at least . . .' The urge for precision overtaking her, 'I did know something was different, but I decided it was just ill health and that the voyage would make me better.'

The baby had worked one arm free of its blanket. Its hand waved hopefully in the air, like some tendril shoot trying to find a gripping place.

'Who was it?' said Allbones.

Eugenia shrugged. 'No one,' she said.

'That's not possible,' said Allbones. 'All babbies has a father.' Stallion to mare, dog to bitch, hob to slut.

Eugenia was silent. Some lad chancing on her in the wood as she was chasing her dragonflies perhaps? Some guest in that big house who had broken into her virginal room as she lay sleeping?

'It doesn't matter,' she said. 'Nothing matters now.'

She lay back against her pillows as her baby opened its pink mouth and began to wail and the midwife at the door bustled in and gathered him up before he could disturb the whole ship.

'At least she was talkin',' the midwife said to her husband as they lay pressed together in their narrow berth, whispering to each other in the early dawn. 'An' not lyin' there like some dead body. An' he seems like a decent enough lad, despite what he's done.'

She had taken the baby to the poor woman who had milk after her own had died. A pretty child who had failed to thrive as the *Adam and Eve* had bucked across the boisterous latitudes and who had expired off this strange coast, only days from landfall. When the woman had been handed this unwanted scrap of a baby her breasts had hardened within minutes and become hot, and the eager clamp of his tough little gums had drawn a gushing of milk from her, along with some of the grief.

'There's no justice, is there?' the midwife whispered to her husband. 'The child that's loved and wanted dies, while the child that's spurned looks set to thrive. He's strong. His mother's too young to know what's what. It'll take a loss or two to teach her.' She sighed. It was hard sometimes to be patient.

Allbones retreated to the deck. He had not long to wait. The next afternoon one of the first-class stewards arrived as he was pouring the dregs from the water barrels into the ferrets' drinking vessels. A varied light passed over the ship, the sails catching a choppy breeze and the coast was clear to port: a landscape of high cliffs topped with patches of forest and cleared land where the passengers could make out small farm-houses and cattle among the blackened stumps of burned trees. The cliffs were streaked with red and from their base stretched sharp ridges of reef and rock, emerging like teeth from the surf. The ship maintained its careful course. More than one voyage had ended in grief just here, the emigrants drowned in their best clothes only a few yards from land. A warm wind blew from the land, bearing the smells of settlement: the rich yeast of leaf mould and damp earth, the milky perfume of cows, the sweet reek of sheep's wool, the incense of wood smoke. The passengers lined the rail and breathed it all in. And in their cages the surviving ferrets brightened. Their eyes began to glisten. They squeaked and nipped playfully at Allbones' fingers as he fed them the last of the pigeons.

'Metcalfe!' said the steward, from the cabin door. 'Mr Pitford wishes to see you.'

Allbones filled another water bowl. It was important to calculate the amount precisely, for there was still the risk of delay should they be held off by an unfavourable wind at the harbour entrance.

The steward clicked his fingers impatiently. '*Now!*' he said.

Allbones set the jug down and followed.

It was almost as it had been in Ledney: Pitford sat at his desk writing among a scatter of papers and books. Allbones took his place on a Turkish rug. The steward discreetly left the room. There were books on shelves and the microscope stood as before on a desk where the light was brightest. The same, yet subtly changed. Shrunken. As before, the older man did not trouble to look up as he entered, nor pause in his writing, but Allbones detected in the studied indifference a kind of pretence. There was anger and bluff in the tremor affecting the writing hand.

'So,' said the older man, glancing up at last and carefully blotting what he had written. 'So, young man, we have something to discuss, do we not?'

'Mebbe we do,' said Allbones. And there was something to his tone that alerted Pitford to look more closely. Before him on the rug stood a man with a certain assurance that was not at all to his liking.

'Young man,' he said, 'I have become aware in the most embarrassing fashion that you, sir, have . . .' He flushed, his jaw tightened with anger.

'. . . have done nothin',' said Allbones. 'I've spoken with your granddaughter, yes. Often. And she has helped with the ferrets. She's fond of animals. But there's been nothin' more.'

'You expect me to believe that?' said Pitford. 'When there have been witnesses to your assignations?'

'I mayn't be much of a scholar,' said Allbones, 'but I can count well enough. I met your granddaughter for the first time, as you well know, eight months ago, when you was out lookin' for badgers. I can count, and I know how long it takes to bear a child. She were already quick, that night.' He looked the other man straight in the eye. 'Someone else made her so.'

Pitford got to his feet and stood before the porthole with his back to the room. Beyond his head Allbones could catch glimpses of the new land, rising and falling as the *Adam and*

Eve surged toward port, a day inside the record and every sail set.

'So,' said Pitford, 'if I am to take your word for it, we must suspect some other scoundrel. I don't suppose in all your conversations with my granddaughter that she has given any hint of whom this villain might be?'

'None,' said Allbones.

'She has told no stories? Mentioned nothing untoward?' said Pitford. 'I should warn you that she is given on occasion to extravagant fancies. Like all young girls, she possesses a romantic and irrational mind.'

'I never heard any fancies,' said Allbones.

'No suggestion that anything might be troubling her?' said Pitford.

'None at all,' said Allbones.

A pause. Pitford sighed deeply.

'A bad business all round,' he said.

A clock ticked, one dial set to Greenwich mean time, the other to the time particular to this longitude. Time passed, in two vastly different realms. At last Pitford seemed to reach a decision.

'A bad business, but it does no good perhaps to agitate over the exact paternity of the child. What's done is done.' He resumed his place behind his desk with something of his former certainty.

Allbones stood upon the rug and waited.

'We must forget the past and plan for the future,' said Pitford. 'What matters now is to find a remedy. We must find a solution to this business which will result in the least harm to one's reputation and the minimum of scandal.'

He reached over and took his pipe from the rack.

'It is impossible, clearly, for my granddaughter to return to England. Too many people have witnessed her shame. Had the birth occurred ashore, at a safe remove from society, concealment might have been possible, the baby disposed of to some colonial wife and Eugenia could have returned to England untainted . . . '

He took a lucifer and struck it.

Allbones was familiar with that solution, too. Some of the girls from Ledney did not remain in the village but left suddenly to visit an aunt in Derbyshire or a cousin at a safe distance for an extended period, returning after an interval, a little pale, perhaps, a little more serious than before.

'But however desirable that may have been, it is no longer possible,' said Pitford. Smoke gathered about his prophetic head. Outside, the ship's wake carved a white path back toward England. Its white furrow formed, then widened to a broad road, then dissolved and vanished. There was no way home.

'I have a proposal to make to you,' said Pitford.

'A proposal?' said Allbones warily.

'Yes,' said Pitford. 'You say you have spoken with my granddaughter.'

'I have,' said Allbones.

'On numerous occasions?' said Pitford.

'Yes,' said Allbones.

'And were these conversations amiable?' said Pitford.

'I believe so,' said Allbones.

'In fact, you might be said to have some kindly feelings toward her?' said Pitford.

Allbones took a deep breath. 'I'm fond of her,' he said.

Pitford's eyes narrowed. Smoke curled about a sunbeam

that fell like a pool of clear water to Allbones' feet.

'And might it be conceivable that these kindly feelings are reciprocated on her part?' said Pitford.

'Mebbe,' said Allbones. 'I think she likes me right enough.'

Pitford mused upon the phrase. 'She likes him "right enough" . . .' he said. He drew deeply on his pipe. 'And he is "fond" of her . . . Her reputation is a wreck, but something might yet be salvaged . . .'

This was Pitford's proposal: that Allbones, although not, perhaps, the father of the child, had been so named before several hundred witnesses. That he might therefore be in a position to agree to becoming the child's father in the eyes of the law by marrying Eugenia, forthwith, before the *Adam and Eve* came into port. He would thereafter undertake to remain with her in the colony where, at some remove from society, a doubtful birth might, in time, be forgotten.

'You seem a steady fellow,' said Pitford. 'You will no doubt quickly make a way for yourself as a worthy citizen. I should, of course, ensure that you are both established comfortably.'

A house. A quarterly remittance. His granddaughter would suffer no indignity.

As for Metcalfe's responsibilities back home? A mere detail. Allowance would be made for any members of his family who might wish to join them in the colony. Every effort would be made to ensure the stability of the union . . .

A sunbeam is dancing over Allbones' toes. The coast slides by outside the little round eye of the porthole. A place where he might live. And Eugenia, her son, Mary Anne, Willie, the littl'uns . . . The light picks out the scarlet thread of the carpet, the tangle of flower and vine.

Meanwhile, in her cabin, Eugenia is rolling over to look at her son. He lies there with his wide blue eyes and his broad brow, making his first observations of the world about him. His arm waves hopefully and she puts out her finger. He grasps it in his tiny pink paw and hangs on tight. She feels his grip and in her stomach there is an uncurling, like something growing. She takes a moment to identify it, but thinks it might conceivably be the beginnings of that sensation she has read about: the one Allbones called 'love'.

9.

It is interesting to contemplate a tangled bank, clothed with many plants of many kinds, with birds singing on the bushes, with various insects flitting about and with worms crawling through the damp earth, and to reflect that these elaborately constructed forms, so different from each other and dependent upon each other in so complex a manner, have all been produced by laws acting around us. These laws taken in the largest sense being Growth with Reproduction; Inheritance, which is almost implied by reproduction; Variability from the indirect and direct action of the conditions of life, and from use and disuse; a Ratio of Increase so high as to lead us to a Struggle for Life, and as a consequence to Natural Selection, entailing Divergence of Character and the Extinction of less-improved forms. Thus, from the war of

> nature, from famine and death, the most exalted
> object which we are capable of conceiving,
> namely the production of the higher animals,
> directly follows.
>
> Charles Darwin, *The Origin of Species*, 1859

Mr and Mrs Metcalfe have come ashore. They are newly married. A simple service aboard ship has been conducted by Captain Scruby in his capacity as chaplain. A short service, according to the rubric of *The Book of Common Prayer*, for although the record for the shortest voyage out has eluded them, there is still some urgency to make port before a summer gale drives them off once more. The crew are eager for the delights of Wellington. The passengers eager to touch land once more.

Mr and Mrs Metcalfe have with them an infant son, whom they have named Walter, perhaps in honour of a fellow countryman who had worked with Mr Metcalfe in the care and maintenance of a consignment of mustelids destined to solve the rabbit problem prevalent in the colony. An odd choice altogether, for Mr Allbones seemed to dislike Mr Metcalfe intensely and made no farewell, simply pocketed his pay and disembarked to join the crowd milling about the quay. When last seen he was enquiring of a slightly puzzled young woman wearing a neatly tailored dress and fashionable hat where the palm trees were. Perhaps she could have enlightened him, had her tram not arrived at that very moment.

So here they come, the little family, seated in the gig that will carry them to their new home beyond the hills. On other wagons, the ferrets follow, their crates stacked four deep for the journey north. Comfort and every convenience await them.

Pitford's cousin has prepared small huts for them on the spurs and valleys of his run and in the bush — the waste ground — at its borders. Pinky travels in the third cage down on the right-hand side of the foremost wagon. Her pink nose whiffles as she smells the sweet deep soil of her new home. She smells feathers and flesh and warm blood. She hears thousands upon thousands of birds singing songs new to her: korimako and tui. Piopio, miromiro, matata, hihi, kakariki, kaka and unsuspecting huia. They bob from branch to branch or peck about the forest floor or soar in the open air. Pinky sits in her cage, her belly rippling already with the next litter. She sniffs and presses her lithe and perfect body against the netting of her cage, eager for release. Not long now.

Eugenia sits beside her husband. The baby is held by its nurse, the woman from the ship whom they have engaged to continue caring for their son. He is a strong child, who will grow sturdy of limb and bright of eye with a healthy appetite and immense vigour. The tide of life runs strongly in him. But then it should, shouldn't it? For as anyone conversant with the scientific breeding of livestock will tell you, the strongest progeny are those fathered by the grandsire. Racehorses and cattlebeasts are bred thus, so why should the laws of genetics be any different for primates? We are just clever monkeys after all, subject to the same regime of natural selection.

The baby's small lungs take in the country's shining air. His eyes attempt focus on its shining leaves, its brilliant sky. He clings with his primate fists to the fringes of his nurse's cloak. The nurse's husband shakes the reins and the horse drawing the gig breaks into a smart trot out along a white gravel road, tossing dust beneath its hooves. They seem a steady couple, the nurse and her husband. Capable, not easily upset. It was wise no doubt to recruit them on board, before the *Adam and Eve* drew into port. The cabin passengers had been warned that it was best to recruit staff then, before the emigrants had taken a whiff of the new conditions prevalent here and begun to make unreasonable demands.

On her own lap, Eugenia holds a cage containing her nightingales. Both have survived the journey and bob about happily, singing snatches. They are beginning to sprout new feathers. When they get to their destination, Eugenia intends to let them free. They will fly from their boxes and make a new home in the bush, where their singing will delight all who pass by. The most romantic music on earth.

The birds do not do that, in the event. Blackbirds thrive here, and thrushes. And the house sparrows released by mistake for hedge sparrows in Lyttelton have produced a mighty progeny that infests farms the length and breadth of the country and must be poisoned. Thousands of their small brown immigrant bodies lie drying to leathery skins among the ripening corn.

Nature's laws are all-powerful. Her clever monkeys cannot anticipate how new organisms will conduct themselves once released into a strange environment.

Eugenia's nightingales, for example. They stay only for that summer. And in the autumn they fly south on their newly feathered wings, seeking in the wide and empty reaches of the Pacific the warm breeding grounds of Africa.

	£	s	d
Allbones' passage money home per 'Ionic'	21	0	0
Telegram 8 words to Agent General	4	13	4
To collect vermin as per			
Agent General's statement rendered	674	13	4
Assistant on voyage out	10	0	0
Allbones, W. wages	40	0	0
Bonus 39 weasels @ 5/- ea.	9	15	0
183 ferrets/stoats/ @ 7/- ea.	64	1	0
	824	2	8

Adapted from February 1885 accounts, Riddiford Papers,
New Zealand National Library

HISTORICAL NOTE

Mr Allbones and Fowler Metcalfe really existed, though nothing is known about them, so far as I am aware, except their names. They appear with a kind of ironical aptness on a couple of receipts for a consignment of stoats ordered in 1885 by the Wairarapa runholder, Edward Riddiford.

Rabbits imported to the colony for sport only a few decades earlier had multiplied alarmingly and were competing with sheep for pasture. Shooting and poisoning were effective on cleared ground but it was believed that the rabbits would retreat and repopulate from bordering 'wasteland' or bush. The solution proposed by experts and landowners, and approved by the government, was to introduce 'their natural predator'.

Hundreds of stoats, weasels and ferrets were imported from Britain at great expense and effort and released into New Zealand's fragile environment, whose bird species — many of them flightless — were already in retreat.

Vast numbers of humans from industrialised Europe were on the move. Those that arrived in New Zealand brought with them religious notions of human supremacy over nature, a fierce determination to reshape the land to fit it for participation in new forms of global trade, and a dispassionate curiosity shaped by that European mode of enquiry called natural science.

The result has been a record of extinctions of bird species without equal anywhere in the world.

SOMETIME IN THE 1860s Harry Head — 'the Hermit of Hickory Bay' — experimented unsuccessfully with flight in an isolated valley on Banks Peninsula. Twelve characters, driven by obsession, hope or the vagaries of chance, come ashore in widely different circumstances onto the same island. Once there, the game can begin.

Written in two halves, *The Hopeful Traveller* is a book to be read from either end. Begin with the past and race toward the future, or begin with the present and circle back towards the past.

'[the] richness — of both theme and languages — imbues it with sometimes startlingly sensual imagery.'

Margie Thomson, NZ Herald

'History, contemporary angst, and a dash of the miraculous — a rich mix.'

Molly Anderson, Otago Daily Times

THE HOPEFUL
TRAVELLER
Fiona Farrell

ONE BOOK, TWO BEGINNINGS – READ FROM EITHER END

AS WAR IS WAGED in the Middle East, a woman in Otago has her nose in a book. Kate is immersed in other battles, engrossed in eyewitness accounts of an earlier war in ancient Persia. She has grown up, left New Zealand and returned, and in all these years books have shaped her life and made sense of the world — offering mystery and solace, entertainment and enlightenment.

In an evocative, moving and frequently funny mix of memoir and fiction, Fiona Farrell writes of life, from *The Little Red Hen* to *Owls Do Cry*, from Enid Blyton to Aphra Behn.

'this is a timely book, tapping into our deepening national awareness of history and identity in which literature plays a huge part.'

Molly Anderson, *Otago Daily Times*

'a little one-of-its-kind masterpiece'

Iain Sharp, *Sunday Star-Times*

'a lovely book, literary and bookish yet totally accessible.'

Margie Thomson, *NZ Herald*

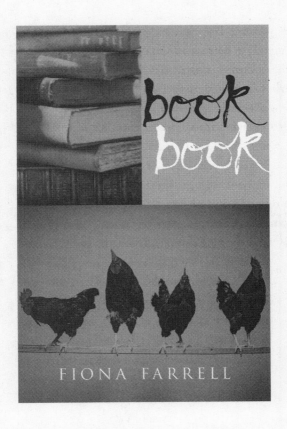

'Book Book is a delightful reaffirmation for bibliophiles for whom books . . . and reading are a central part of their being and identity.'

Philippa Barrett, *Bookshelf*